PERFIDY

(Betrayal)

By

Ra Dee

ISBN:

Ebook: 979-8-90224-049-5

Paperback: 979-8-90224-050-1

Hardcover: 979-8-90224-051-8

Published by:

Authors Publishing House

178 Broadway, 3rd Floor, #1343

New York, NY 10001, USA

Main Line: (855) 624-0155

Email: support@authorspublishinghouse.com

Dedicated To My Wife Rose

Whose unselfish love provided

me with three years of unparalleled

Happiness

Introduction

The actual name of this governmental entity is unpronounceable in any earthly language. For the sake of clarity, it will be called "Empire". Also, many names, places, and items have sounds that have no equivalent in our human language, so for better understanding, I will make approximations to the sounds. Most items mentioned will be terms understandable by the reader. However, there are some that are difficult to describe except by what they are called. I will attempt to describe these as well as possible. Times are varied from place to place because of different orbits and rotations of the varied planets involved; therefore, for simplicity, I will use a standard of time based on the orbit and rotation of this earth, and I will refer to them as people or persons.

In a far-off area of space, there is a galaxy consisting of perhaps a thousand or more solar systems, barely visible with even the most powerful telescopes and sophisticated instruments on this planet. There is a system called, by those living in the system, Zazabukna. From the sun of this system, the fourth planet is called Traket, the ONLY fully inhabited planet of that solar system.

Those living on this planet walk upright, bipedal, and are highly progressed in domestic, scientific, and military operations, plus they are very aggressive in nature. They attained space flight centuries before humans began to consider the wheel. They explored their own system, colonizing as many areas as possible before attempting to venture out of their own system.

This is the story of those "peoples", the problems encountered in the expansion of what they considered their destiny for "more living space."

Background

Initially, it was determined that it would take centuries to reach the nearest star system, and anyone sent would never be heard from again; therefore, a faster method had to be developed BEFORE the first explorers. A faster method was developed, but would still require multiple tens of years before the first explorers could be sent, along with a small contingent of colonists, and return. The intention was that the explorers, trained with military weapons and tactics, would protect and help settle the colonists and then return to Traket with a report and for more colonists. The explorers carried weapons believed capable of protecting the colonists, and a small contingent would remain to protect the colonists until the next group of explorers and colonists returned.

The first attempt would consist of six different groups, two ships for each group, and the destination for each group would be a different star system. The thought was that, in the unlikely event of some unforeseen difficulty, the odds of more groups returning were thus increased.

Although the faster method of travel was developed, the time between systems would require multiple tens of years. A further refinement would later reduce the time to years, then months, and finally days, but that was still centuries in the future.

The first dozen or more ships sent did not return as programmed and, for reasons undetermined, had not returned or heard from again. Future flights were cancelled, but not before another group of twenty ships had been built.

Several reasons were considered, ranging from departing navigational problems, such as the group actually ending in the same position as another celestial body, entering the wrong system, to inhabitants of the planet more powerful than thought, the navigation difficulties of not being able to find the home system, and several other problems not anticipated. Until these possible problems and many others could be resolved, all excursions beyond their system had to be halted; the expenditure of money, time, and training of personnel was tremendous, without obtaining a return on investment.

The population of Traket continued to increase, and with the increase came unrest because of these huge expenditures of time, money, and material without any noticeable return to improve the standard of living or, as promised, travel to other systems and be given FREE land for any and all who would like it. Natural resources began to be scarce and expensive, and with the rise in prices for even basic necessities, the population began to be restless and discouraged.

The unrest became uprisings, which in turn erupted into outright rebellion. The rebellion expanded into a war between the government and several different factions of the population. A civil war was now full-blown as portions of the military seceded from the government along with their weapons, and many of the areas in rebellion were the areas that produced the weapons for the government. The war expanded into space and into the colonized areas. The war became brutal as one faction fought to gain control of important but scarce resources, only to lose them in another furious battle with another faction or the government. As one faction might be subdued, another faction would arise, and so the war continued for over two centuries.

With the huge loss of individuals, material, military craft, and transport ships, plus much of the expertise needed to build and maintain a space fleet, the population as a whole withdrew from space and regressed into an almost primitive stage of existence. Without adequate spacecraft to move resources or supplies, those that had survived on the colonized planets, asteroids, and satellites of the system were without any outside support. The replenishment of needed supplies and additional colonists dwindled to nothing; soon, survivors began to die off, leaving only uninhabited sites scattered around the solar system. Even the sites, after years of disrepair and disuse, began to crumble.

It took several centuries for the population to grow, and it began to venture once more into space. Many of the previous gains before the war had been forgotten; there was only what was indicated in some ancient writings, which made little sense to most of the present population. With only these widely scattered bits and pieces of written information, which had somehow survived, when found, they gave little if any at all hint of the previous colonists and explorers. The records of the advances in the previous technology were almost all completely destroyed; most had to be "learned "again, until a few enterprising individuals gathered as many of the fragments as possible and began to piece together the information about space flight.

The previous explorers and colonists who had traveled outside the Zazabukna system, information about them or their possible fate had survived only in the smallest of fragments, and even when all put together, it was not enough to make any understandable sense.

These explorers and colonists had adapted, changed, and even mutated to their environments. Although still walking upright, few resembled the original colonists, and none knew anything or cared about Traket; those memories had dimmed and finally vanished as generation after generation developed and adjusted to the environment and living conditions of the only planet THEY knew.

The changes were many and varied, depending on a multitude of factors such as distance from their sun, the gravitational force of the planet, diet, and even the air they breathed. There were so many factors that it was understandable the first "visitors" from Traket were considered aliens. The only thing vaguely similar was that they walked upright, and perhaps a few of the words spoken. The inability to understand or be understood, made the "visitors", only not welcome but resulted in furious battles to expel the "invaders".

Those from Traket, the biggest problem of which they considered was to overcome the time/ distance problem, and a means of communication before the first ships left their own system. The present population, severely decimated in all the wars, was in no hurry to explore outside their own system. The time/distance was first considered and finally reduced to a little over a year to the nearest system, and navigation was next; it had to be precise. They wanted to be able to communicate with the explorers, so they set relay buoys on the outer perimeter of their system. Actually, communication would still require a longer period of time to receive than the actual flight, but it was thought necessary. Now they believed they were ready to begin the exploration outside their own system.

They were determined to expand their territory and influence, regardless of whom or what might be in the way. The reason given was the need for "growing" space. The first attempt ended in disaster. The group encountered inhabitants with powerful weapons and was unprepared to confront any entity with weapons of the same or greater firepower than their own. Another factor not carefully considered by those from Traket was fighting, which developed. The inhabitants of the planet involved knew the territory; it WAS their home, and they, as invaders, did not realize or take into account the environmental and even the gravitational differences between the two systems. What operated well on Traket did not operate the same way elsewhere.

The name of the first planet to be thus engaged, they learned, was Thergotis. The individuals were of short stature, pale brown, and had high physical strength. They had adapted to a higher gravity and a lower oxygen level of the planet, and a food supply of lower nutritional value than that on Traket. The Thergots had expanded their jurisdiction from the main planet to several other areas within the system, colonizing for extra-needed raw materials. It was from one of these sites that the first detected the force from Traket entering the system and alerted the main planet. The main planet was ready to repulse the "invaders".

The first excursion limped back to Traket, badly mauled. The second attempt would be conducted with an overwhelming force of arms. To ensure success, a very small scout ship would return and attempt to land unnoticed with spies. Although noticed, the spies were able to determine several important factors and relay the information back before being killed, either by the inhabitants or self-inflicted; however, the damage was done.

The invasion force left the Zazabukna system with a massive force of six huge battle cruisers and a large contingent of support craft. The invading force was aware of the physical adaptations of the Thergos, as they were called; however, they also believed they needed to push out of the way to attain "growing space".

Aware that there would be a returning force, the belief that they had defeated it once and could do it again, there was no idea of its size until it appeared.

A fierce battle began, the military on both sides was neutralized into a stalemate, but not without huge casualties and loss of material on both sides, especially on the invading force due to the battles taking place in the higher gravity. Their weapons did not function with the accuracy and efficiency as on Traket. Through the use of individuals captured from several battles, the language of each was learned, and finally, a peace treaty was offered. From these captures, similarities between the two became apparent. Peace terms were accepted by both, and the Goths were absorbed into the "Empire". It was later that more similarities were found, and they began to think that they were possible descendants of Traket. Because of this, the inhabitants were offered full membership into the "Empire" with all of its advantages and benefits. Accepted by many, there were still those who would not accept anyone they considered to be an invader. This required a military force to remain on the planet to subdue the rebels and protect those accepting the treaty and from any other "invaders".

The advantage of membership was representation in the government and unrestricted trade, but it also required the acceptance of colonists from Traket. Many colonists came but could not adjust to the environment, and just as many left. That left only the military to contend with the "rebels"; the losses were lopsided in favor of the rebels. The military also had the same problem as did the first colonists sent from Traket: the adjustment to the new environment. The ones living here had centuries to adjust.

Moving on to the next possible objective, still looking for more space to expand, the next system was called Rettusbic. The Rettuses were different from the previous inhabitants of Thergotis. The Rettuses were very close to the size of the Trakets, with a pale, almost sickly color of gray, longer arms and legs, and thin in stature but very robust and aggressive. The gravity of Rettusbic was less than that of Traket; the terrain was rocky with sparse vegetation, numerous mountain ranges, and was cooler because of the distance from the sun. The majority of the food supply grew over six feet above the ground; very little that was usable for food grew at a lower level.

The invaders again had large losses, the inherited aggressive nature of the Rettuses, almost continuous rough terrain encountered, no visible central population centers were the major reasons. The advantage of remaining outside the atmosphere and bombarding any center of activity was nullified.

The Rettuses had adapted to living inside the mountainous terrain, and a series of interconnecting tunnels produced towns and cities under the mountains. Each habitation had to be found and occupied one by one by ground troops. The conquering of this planet was both extremely expensive and time-consuming, and was never completely accomplished. The fact that there was NO central government hampered the signing of any kind of treaty. It was only AFTER a large number of the individual "cities" were subdued that representatives from Traket assisted the Rettuses to establish a loose form of government around these cities, gradually adding others until a majority, or at least thought to be a majority, were offered admission into the "Empire". However, it was an uneasy "peace". It was left to the officials of the newly formed "government" to convince the other scattered cities to join the government and the Empire. Again, because of this, a large "occupation" force was needed to keep order. For Traket, a better, less expensive, and easier way HAD to be found.

A committee was formed to find a way to subdue the various populations without the huge expense of an armed invasion and occupation, which was not ONLY costly in loss of personnel and material of the invasion but also in maintaining the occupation forces needed afterward. As the Empire expanded and time/distance factors became more acute, the need for a better and less expensive alternative grew in direct proportion to expansion. The committee, consisting of the most intelligent and forward-thinking individuals possible, was assembled.

As even within the population of Earth, there were and are certain individuals with greater abilities than the general population. Called child prodigies or geniuses, they seem to have knowledge and or abilities above and beyond what is considered normal. Within the populations of the "integrated" planets, there were also those whose abilities were far enhanced above the "normal".

This committee began by recruiting individuals from the three different planets, the very best available from each planet. It was found that each of the inhabitants from Thergotic and Rettusric had certain abilities and capabilities not found on Traket, and still others of the population had these abilities that were even greater.

As the group grew and problems were presented, many ideas were introduced, some outright rejected, and others carefully considered. After much discussion and debate, it was agreed that the solution was to somehow have a group, answerable to the government, the Emperor in particular, but if questioned, not recognized by the government. It would have to be very secretive, work undercover, disrupt the government, if one were found, of the intended target, so that it could be peacefully assumed by specially trained officials of the government of Traket. These would establish order out of the chaos and thus perhaps avoid the expense of military action and occupation. The largest problem considered was an advanced group of individuals to learn about the people and their language, possibly to communicate fluently, and generally learn about the planet itself. This advanced group would openly establish a relationship of trade and assistance with the governmental entity available.

The secret group that would cause the chaos would simply be called "The Organization". It would be financed by the government, accountable to the government, the Emperor in particular, but not recognized by the government in the event of discovery. It would consist of "Special" individuals, trained for infiltration and subversive tactics, utilizing, if possible, any of the special abilities of present or future acquisitions to the "Empire." The idea was submitted to the Emperor, was approved, and put into action.

By the time the "Organization" was sufficiently trained and armed, the Empire had acquired other planets with a huge expenditure of finances, personnel, and material. The individuals of the "Organization" were what we on earth would call mercenaries, but are simply called agents in this "Empire". Before assigning the object to the "Organization", the preliminaries of gaining confidence and learning the language could take months to a year.

The object was to infiltrate the subject planet and, under the guise of rebels and misfits, attack the hierarchy of the government and eliminate as many of the leaders as possible. The chaos and confusion that followed would be enough for official representatives from Traket to offer assistance in recovery. The assistance would also include acceptance into the Empire for stability and "special" protection. The protection would prevent the return of the "marauders".

With success, the advantage for the Empire was no armed invasion and a very minimal occupation afterward, and the cost, including the special equipment and training involved, was considerably less than the outfitting of one battle cruiser.

The very nature of the work required the utmost secrecy; no one was to know when or where an operation was to take place, and until the last possible moment, until official orders were issued. All orders came directly from the "office" of the Emperor. A briefing on the people, government, etc., in question was normally given to the agents while en route to the objective.

There became a requirement for a special communication network, with its own codes and code words designed to transmit an entire sentence or a little more with a single word or symbol. Special scientists and engineers were needed to design the weapons, modes of transportation, electronics, and even miniature explosive devices. Everything needed had to be carried into an operation by the agent, and it had to be easily carried but deadly in use. Included was a device implanted in every agent for easier and continuous access. They were an infra-red detector, which, with a blink of the eye, could receive the heat signature of anything emitting heat. There was an infra-red shield which was not implanted but carried as a small box-like device, activated or turned off by a small switch.

There were five teams organized, and each team of agents included doctors, who went on every operation in the event of an agent being wounded. The doctors remain secluded in an area accessible to the agents but away from the actual operation. With five teams, it would allow one to be on a mission while the other four were resupplied and/or resting prior to the next mission.

The general population of Traket was very vaguely aware of the "Organization," but also knew not to become very interested. They did observe certain individuals suddenly disappear and not be seen for months, if at all, later, and when they did return, seemingly do nothing for an extended length of time before once more disappearing.

The agents were very well paid for their service; many had two or more different places of residence in various areas of Traket. Many had electronic devices installed in and around the property to discourage any curious thrill-seekers or even someone by accident discovering the residence.

Finally, I will use only one name to identify the characters of this story; many of the actual names are long and complicated to pronounce.

With this background, *PERFIDY* begins several centuries AFTER the last armed invasion of a planet.

Table of Contents

I

In the darkness of the night, he found a place to make himself as comfortable as possible. His name, Stafic, a male from the planet Zephinom, referred to as a Zephic, believed to be the last of his species, with light blue skin, extremely quick reflexes, stealthy, and hired by the "Organization" as a night fighter. He had become one of its top agents but is now engaged in a life or death struggle with his partner of over five years, a female, Maradish.

Maradish, a female from the planet Tyrunic, commonly called a Tyrakos, is totally black with not one trace of white or any other color on her; even her eyes have no white in them. Very warlike and aggressive, she is a MASTER of stealth, the only species allowed, by treaty, to carry weapons in the open. The last planet to be engaged in an armed invasion by Traket, never actually subdued, fought to a stalemate, thus a treaty HAD to be negotiated. The Empire could NOT afford to permit such an aggressive and combative population to remain unrestricted within the lines of communication to interrupt "progress".

Maradish and Stafic began an association over eleven years ago when they were sent on an operation together. From the first meeting, it appeared there was a compatibility not shared with any other agent. It appeared, at least to others, that they were able to read the mind of the other; of course, there was no truth to this. Both very quickly rose to be the top agents because of this unique ability. They became very close over the years of being on several operations together, and about five years ago, they began an intimate relationship. Now, for some reason unknown to him, she was trying to kill him.

He HAD to find the reason or die in the attempt!

For Stafic, it would, no doubt, be a long night. Traket had no moon; the only light available for now was starlight and the faint, dim light of the city a distance away. To be able to see one of the most stealthy individuals in the Empire would take every ounce of his skill and a lot of luck; night was her best ally, and where she was the most comfortable.

As he made himself as comfortable as possible, he withdrew the only weapon he had a chance to escape with, a small handheld weapon of short range. Normally used only for close encounters and is usually a means of delaying the opponent long enough to escape. Although it could be deadly within its limited range, its effectiveness quickly dissipates into nothing more than a sting or nothing. By contrast, he was sure she would have a longer-range weapon. She could remain outside the range of his weapon with very little effort.

The only other items on his person were a medical kit and his personnel, Kafari, a double-bladed razor-sharp knife. The Kafari was the only reminder from his teenage years on his home planet, and he carried it on his person at all times and was even close by when he was asleep.

With the small weapon in hand, he carefully set it with two clicks, medium stun, two more upward clicks, and it would kill. One click down, it would only sting like a bee. He wanted only to stun her, if possible, both because of their very close relationship, and he needed to know why she was so intent on killing him. There were two problems that were upfront and important; one was to see her before she saw him. If this were not possible, he was as good as dead. Two, to see her and she be within range of his weapon. If either one was not possible, any other problem would be mute.

He opened his eyes as wide as possible to allow as much of the dim light to enhance any shadows, and he had to keep moving his eyes; to focus on any one object would tend to make THAT object appear to move, which would be deadly for him. He had, as he was sure she had also, his infra-red shield on and his infra-red sensor activated. With all of them activated, any advantage was neutralized; therefore, only a visual contact of detection would have to be used.

He remained quiet, moving his head as little as possible, just enough to bring another area into view. He had to try to keep the position of shadows in mind so if any were different, it MAY indicate where she might be, remembering all the while she WAS a master at stealth and was very capable of suddenly being within arms reach before known to be close, by the time it is realized, IT IS too late! His only advantage was that he knew this and maybe, just maybe, somehow could make an allowance for it.

A disadvantage was that she knew him and he knew her so well, they should easily be able to predict the next move the other will make. He had to quickly think of something she may not expect, something he had never done before; what that could be is most elusive at present. The only possible thing might be a diversion, but what? Diversion? Many years ago, on his home planet, as a child during the exercise periods, it was always a tactic to try to make your opponent "think" you were someplace you were not.

Slowly and carefully, inch by inch, he searched for a rock; it had to be big enough to make a noise but small enough to toss. He felt the ground very slowly, all the while watching for any shadow that was not there before. After what appeared to be hours of searching, inch by inch, he found one small stone. It was not the size he would have liked, but it would have to do. At least he hoped it would be adequate. Now he had to somehow get the stone into a position where he could use it, without much movement or especially noise.

It would begin to be daylight in about three hours; her biggest asset and security would disappear, IF he could only survive that long. It could possibly be the longest three hours of his life.

He waited, scanning the surroundings for anything out of place or any movement, no matter how slight or slow. At least there was no breeze; he might be able to detect movement of leaves, IF any of them moved.

Everything was so quiet and still, his mind began to wander. "What happened to cause this radical change in her behavior? It happened about three months ago. Whatever had happened, she was not thinking, acting, or even reacting like the professional he knew she was. If that was a fact, she may make a mistake, however slight, and he would HAVE to be ready to take immediate action. His reaction had to be instantaneous, quick, and accurate. He had to be ready; perhaps the diversion would help, maybe?" He had to stop allowing his mind to wander and concentrate on the present; whatever had happened would be useless if he did not survive the night.

Two hours to sunrise, a lot could happen in two hours. He could only wait, stay as quiet as possible; it was boring, and his muscles began to ache. He wanted to move to relieve the aches, but his training had taught him to remain motionless or face detection and death.

What seemed like an eternity, suddenly, very close to him and to his right, "Stafic!" The sound of her voice, so close and loud, startled him and almost caused him to flinch. "I know you are here." She continued, "We need to talk!"

That was not like her to even give a hint of her position. Perhaps she believed, and rightly so, that he would not harm her, or maybe whatever was causing the change in attitude was affecting her ability to think clearly. Whatever the reason, he had to remain quiet

"Please talk to me," She pleaded with a sadness in her voice which almost broke his heart. "I love you. I would do nothing to hurt you." The sound of her concern almost made him jump and run to her. With much restraint, he HAD to control himself; if he did not, he would not know about it seconds later.

He saw a small movement, a brief shadow. Too quick and small to be able to hit with his weapon with any kind of accuracy, a better target HAD to present itself! His next move would require a lot of luck; if she happened to be looking his direction, he would not be alive long enough to know the difference.

With as little movement of his arm as possible, he threw the stone as far as possible to his right and far enough away, he hoped, to make a noise away from him. In a high arc as possible, it would maybe land and make enough noise to have her look away from his position.

The stone landed with a soft sound, as if someone had stepped on a leaf or very small twig. The sound was sufficient; a bright blue streak of light flashed through the darkness and hit the area of the sound. He knew from the color of the flash that she had her weapon set to kill!

He remained absolutely quiet. He realized from the color of the streak of light that whatever it hit would cause an instantaneous death without a sound from the person, except maybe, if standing, the body falling to the ground.

With the sun beginning to rise, and he knew her approximate location, he also knew she would have to investigate to "make sure" the job was complete. He watched for any kind of movement, of any shadow or anything that appeared to be out of place. He saw a slight movement. She was slowly approaching the area of the shot. He quickly shot his weapon, an orange streak of light flashed, it hit the shadow, and the shadow crumbled to the ground with a soft groan.

He now had to move fast; the stun would only last a short time, and if she was faking the collapse, the next flash would be his last he would ever see, but he had to take that chance.

He quickly found her; she was lying very still, on her side, still holding her weapon in her hands. If she was faking, it would be all over very shortly; he had to move quickly. He withdrew from the medicine kit a syringe and a vial containing a green liquid. He filled the syringe about a quarter of the way and injected the liquid into her arm.

When on a mission, this was used on a captured opponent for interrogation. It only caused a temporary immobility, but in this case, it should allow him time to disarm her and hopefully get her back to his vehicle, where he had other medicines that would prolong the time and allow enough time to get her to his apartment. He had to move fast; if the effects of the liquid wore off before he could get her further sedated, he would have a lot of trouble trying to control her. Once in the apartment, he had a much safer sedative he could use, which he used on himself, mainly when returning from a mission to relieve the aches and pains of the mission.

He threw her over his shoulder and ran as fast as possible through the trees and back to where he had left his air-car. As he ran toward the location of the air-car, he could only hope she had not disabled it, as they often did opponents' vehicles when on a mission. If she did, then he would have to find where she might have placed hers, which could be anywhere. He could, but did not want to give her another injection of this sedative; her body metabolism was such that it could easily kill her. Those from Tyrakos were very sensitive to many drugs, among them, sedatives, one at the apartment would be more acceptable to her metabolism.

He ran to his air-car, placed her in the passenger side, and sat down on his side. With the code words, the engine sprang to life. Again, this was another indication she was not acting in the way she had been trained or to think. She should have disabled the vehicle, or maybe she thought she would be walking out by herself and would do it then, or just leave it abandoned. He didn't have time to analyze the possibilities; he had to get her to the apartment before she was awake enough to cause any problems. It was all very puzzling, but maybe he would be able to figure it out later.

With another very small injection, he set the coordinates on the computer system, the controls on maximum speed, avoidance, and guidance to his apartment. He pressed the activation button, and the air-car roared into the air, quickly attaining a speed of over a hundred miles an hour into the rising sun.

Every agent of the "Organization" had their own private vehicle. The governor, standard equipment to control the speed of all air vehicles produced, had been removed. At his request, the engineers had added special equipment to increase speed beyond the speed of "normal" ones, and with pinpoint guidance and avoidance systems, it made his vehicle uniquely exclusive.

With mental calculations, he determined that he would be at the apartment in less than five minutes, which would give him less than two minutes to get her inside the apartment and secured before she began to awaken. He had to have her secured; she was very dangerous if not secured before she was fully awake.

Slightly more than four minutes later, the air-car came to a stop in front of the apartment building. He quickly exited the car and rushed around to the other side to remove her. As he lifted her out and cradled her in his arms, he noticed several neighbors watching. Many were leaving for work and looked at the couple with smiles and perhaps thought they were returning from some all-night party. He saw their looks, so he acted sheepishly to reinforce the thoughts or ideas in their mind.

Not wanting to engage anyone in any type of conversation, not that any of them would, and rather than take the chance, he rushed into the apartment building with her in his arms and to his apartment, which was on the first floor. He had to release one arm, her feet hit the floor, but she was still supported with the other arm, he entered the codes, and the door opened. Once inside, the door would close automatically. Once more, he threw her over his shoulders and hurried inside. As he entered, she began to groan and move. He hurried into the bedroom. Placing her on the bed, he retrieved a kit from the side table, quickly took a syringe and a small bottle of pink liquid. With only a very small amount in the syringe, he injected the liquid into her arm, and she almost immediately became limp again. The amount injected was only enough for her to completely relax, not enough to cause unconsciousness. This sedative would allow him about two to three minutes to secure her. First, he needed to return to the entry door to reset the keypad and alarm system.

With the keypad and alarm set, he returned to the bedroom. She appeared to be starting to move, which meant he would have to hurry; the sedative may be wearing off faster than he expected, or he may be being cautious. He had not administered enough. He quickly removed all her clothing, nude, he secured her to the bed and began the search over her body for the hidden devices she had on her person, which, if she was ever captured, she would use to escape any device used to secure her. Satisfied, he stood up from his labor in time to see her eyes begin to flutter; she was waking up.

In less than thirty seconds, she groaned and looked at him. She attempted to move and discovered she was firmly attached to the bed. "Wha.. Why am I tied down?" She groaned.

"We need to talk, and I don't want you trying to kill me as we do, " he replied.

"I am not trying to kill you. Turn me loose so we can talk about why you would think such a thing."

"I'll turn you loose when I have answers and not one second before."

"Well! I am not going to tell you anything until you turn me loose," She growled defiantly.

"I thought you might say that, so I will have to use another method of finding what I need to know." He reached into the drawer of the table next to the bed and withdrew a vial of pale blue liquid.

The pale blue liquid was used on their missions when they needed to interrogate someone and know it was the truth. The liquid had to be administered by body weight; too little was ineffective, and too much was deadly. For Stafic, it would be little trouble to determine; he knew almost exactly how much Maradish weighed.

Still defiant, she said, "You won't DARE use that, you love me too much!"

"Yes, I do love you, but I WILL use it, my love would have no use to you or me if I'm dead."

"I don't want you dead, I LOVE YOU! You are letting your imagination run away with you!" Her voice was no longer defiant but was now filled with a sense of apprehension and panic.

He calmly began to partially fill the syringe with the liquid. He had to be very careful, with her lack of tolerance, it was very critical, just enough should be injected.

Her eyes became very wide as he turned toward her with the needle. "NO! NO!" She screamed as the needle was pushed into her arm. Almost instantly, with her eyes wide open, her breathing became labored, and suddenly she became completely limp.

Stafic waited a few seconds to make sure she was breathing OK and then said, "Mara. Mara, do you hear me?"

"YE....Yees… I hear you."

"Do you really love me?"

"YES, I really love you."

"I am going to ask you some questions. I want you to answer all my questions. Will you do that?"

"Yes. What is it you want to know?"

"When did we first meet?"

"We were on assignment to Jejquen."

"How long have we known each other?"

"Eleven years and four months."

"What is the name of our team leader?"

"Taygo."

" Why do you want to kill me?"

"I don't want to kill you, but it is the pain."

"What pain is that?"

"The pain that I have."

"What kind of pain?"

"A hard, throbbing pain."

"What is causing the pain?"

"He is."

"Who is he?"

"The one causing the pain."

"Can you tell me who is causing the pain?"

"He is."

"Who is he?"

"The one causing the pain."

Believing he would get nowhere with this questioning, he asked, "Where is the pain?"

"In my head."

The injection was beginning to wear off, so he decided to stop the questions; it may take a professional to find the answers. He gave her another very mild sedative and sat back. He suddenly realized he had had nothing to eat for a very long time. During a mission, he may not eat or drink anything for up to two days, but would be famished as soon as it was over.

HE slowly got up, turned the lights to dim, adjusted the door, which had a mirror on it, so he could watch her while he ate, and went into the next room to prepare something to eat. It had been a long night, and he began to rehearse the events in his mind to try to find an answer. He would HAVE to call for assistance. Doctors were very good at arriving at a proper solution, IF they actually believed him. It would be his word against hers; all she would have to do is deny everything. After all, agents support each other, NEVER oppose. Then there was the suspension HE had almost a year ago, directly involving her. Even if it was in anger and in retaliation for an injury she sustained, the action he took indicated a lack of self-control.

He made himself a Varit and to drink, an Oqni. It was not anything like a big piece of Alt'eri and a Umerali he used to have on his own planet. Unfortunately, those no longer exist. The scientists have tried to duplicate, but without the exact ingredients, in the right proportions, it was tasty, but nothing like the real thing.

His mind began to reflect back on how exactly he had reached this point in his life. He thought, it all started, what seemed so long ago, he and a group of his friends had come to Traket to attend a school on how to increase the productivity of the farm. The school was several months in duration, and upon completion, his friends had returned to the home planet to begin the instruction of these NEW procedures. As the designated leader, he stayed to attend an additional four-week course in management and government procedures, especially the paperwork involved.

Not even halfway through the course, the instructor entered the classroom and said to him, "There is no reason for you to continue unless you want." When asked why, he was informed, "Alien marauders have destroyed the entire surface of your planet, there are no known survivors except you, and the planet is little more than a barren rock. They may have taken prisoners to be slaves, but there is no way of knowing it for a fact. We can only take for granted that YOU are the only survivor of your species. You are welcome to remain here, and every attempt will be made to find suitable work for you. We realize this is a shock, take a week or so, and let us know how we may assist."

He had left the classroom and, with his mind in a swirl and fog at the news, began to wander about the city. Grief was almost overwhelming for him, and therefore, he paid little attention to where he was walking. He suddenly heard jeering and words being yelled at him; he had walked into the less desirable part of the city. The jeers and harsh words were being yelled at him from five individuals who appeared to be about his age.

He had paid little attention until he realized he was surrounded. Blocked in every direction when he attempted to move out of their way, the five moved in closer, closing a ring around him in an effort to prevent any possible way of escape.

"Leave me alone, I am not bothering you!" He had said, still attempting to move away from the closing ring of youths.

"OH! He says he is not bothering us. Just being here bothers us. RIGHT guys?"

"YEAH!" They all shouted in chorus.

It was about then that one of them swung at him with a knife, causing only a small cut through his clothing and on the arm. Only his quick reflexes prevented a more serious injury. Before the knife had finished its movement, his Kafari was out of its sheath, and the grief and despair exploded like a volcano. Each side of the blade was slicing in both directions, screams and cursing were heard as one after another fell to the ground, screaming. It was over in a matter of seconds, and he stood in the middle of five crying and bleeding young men.

As he stood looking at the mayhem around him, he saw another individual quickly leave the gathering crowd, walking very quickly and directly toward him. He took a defensive position, but the individual, who appeared to be a pale, male with slightly stooped shoulders, raised his hands to show he had no weapon and said, "You need to get out of here, quick, before the crowd recovers from the shock and the Law arrives. They will not believe you if you say it was self-defense." The pale male held out a card, "Take this card, follow the directions to the address on the card, and use the card for access. The card will self-destruct in fifteen minutes; you have that long to make a decision. So long and good luck." The male disappeared into the crowd.

Believing retreat was the better course of action, he could hear the approaching sirens of the LAW. He took the advice of the pale, stoop-shouldered male and quickly left the scene of bloody teens and hurried away using the directions to the address on the card.

It took over ten minutes, while dodging the LAW, to find the building. It was what would be referred to as a nondescript building, very plain and drab. He stood outside, wondering what it was and if he should even consider going inside. That was when he heard the distinct sounds of the approaching LAW, and again believing retreat was the better option, went to the door and inserted the card in a slot. There was no doorknob or handle on the outside to open the door, but the door opened. Walking through the door, he entered a room with no furniture and only another door on the opposite side.

Inside, the door closed behind him. Startled, he turned to see if there was a way of escape. As he did, a voice suddenly said, "Greetings, my name is not important as is your name. The only thing important is the decision you MUST make in the next two minutes. The decision is which door you will use. The door you entered will allow you to leave with no questions asked; the opposite door, if you enter, you will become a member of an organization. As a member of this organization, you will not be allowed any contact or communication with any and all previous individuals you know. The fact will be, anyone known by you will be told you have been killed, and even ashes will be presented if it is the custom of your species. If you accept those conditions, you have one minute and thirty seconds to use the card in the door you entered or the one opposite; in either case, the card will be destroyed, and the only way out of the room WILL be the way you entered. This is the only message you will hear."

The room suddenly became very quiet. With the thought, there is nothing out the door just entered except possibly conflict with the LAW, he inserted the card into the opposite door and walked through and into a different way of life.

Suddenly, his thoughts were disturbed when he heard a muffled sound from the bedroom. Maradish must have started to awaken; he got up to go to her, and he saw a small flash of light in the mirror. His first thought was that it was Maradish moving, but then he could see her lying very still. An intruder? How could it be an intruder? He said to himself, There is no way an intruder can bypass his security devices. Then in the mirror, he saw a movement, only a shadow, he could still see Maradish, she was still quiet on the bed. Someone else was in the room, and someone had somehow defeated his sophisticated alarm system! But how?

No time to think about THAT, he quickly determined to apprehend whoever it was and determine the answers later. With his weapon in hand, he made sure it was only on stun. He began to move slowly toward the bedroom. The shadow appeared to be moving around Maradish; Maradish seemed to be NOT the reason for the intrusion. The shadow must have also been watching the mirror because with a sudden move, it was behind the only chair in the room. Stafic continued to slowly approach the doorway, but the shadow was no longer visible; therefore, he would have to try to draw the shadow out and into the open.

Maybe the shadow did not know he was seen and could not see him in the mirror at present, and was simply waiting for him to enter the doorway. There was a lot of maybes. He wished now that he had left the lights on full; no sense thinking about what he should have done. He had to concentrate on the problem at hand. With a blink of his eye, he activated the implanted infra-red sensor. No image appeared; could it be that the shadow had an infrared shield? If that were so, then he could very possibly be dealing with an agent or some other equally trained professional? The next move apparently had to be his. With caution and determination, he approached the doorway. His next move left very little room for error. It could mean the difference between life and death for him or whether or not an injury may happen to Maradish.

He gathered his strength and, with a sudden leap and shout, flew through the doorway. As he was still airborne, he fired two quick shots at the last known position of the shadow. The first ripped a hole through the chair, the second followed, striking the floor and ripping and tearing a hole in the floor, carpet, and wood, flying into the air. The space was empty. Whoever was the shadow must have anticipated the move and had quickly and very quietly moved to a different location. As Stafic rolled across the floor and into a firing position, the shadow fired a shot, and a blue streak came from another area. The weapon was set to kill, but the shot missed Stafic by only inches. Stafic moved to avoid the next shot, but the next shot did not materialize. In the split second it took to adjust, the shadow had disappeared through the only window in the room. Unable to get a clear shot at the fleeing shadow, Stafic was left to wonder how it had defeated his security devices, anticipated his move, and still escaped without even a glimpse to be able to identify or even be sure if it was a male or a female that was involved.

With the sounds of discharging weapons, he knew the LAW would soon arrive, and he did not want to be held or restricted by all the questions he was sure would come. With a very small amount of pain medicine injected once more into the arm of Maradish, he removed the restraints, wrapped her still nude body in a blanket, and hurriedly carried her out of the apartment and onto his air bike instead of the air car. The air bike was faster and harder to see both visually and on any radar of the LAW.

As the air bike roared to life and lifted off the ground, he set the controls for the coordinates of his cabin in the woods, maximum speed, and avoidance system on. He selected the emergency frequency, keyed the radio, and spoke in a very carefully worded and calm voice, "X-ray! X-ray! Post alpha four banner two delta thirty one six by fourteen four." Translated, it announced there had been a breach in security, and he was heading to specific coordinates, and a physician was needed. At the speed he was traveling, it would be slightly more than six minutes to the cabin.

The air car streaked through the city, the avoidance system swerving around the buildings, adjusting the speed and altitude to avoid any other vehicles. The speed of his air car was nearly twice the speed of any other vehicle, including the LAW. Less than two minutes later, he cleared the city, the LAW, he believed would not follow, they would not be able to intercept because of the speed, and would not know which direction he might be traveling.

Clear of the buildings, he could relax somewhat and began to reflect on the events that had happened.

Nothing he had seen or done in the past twenty-four hours made any sense. Why was Maradish and whoever that shadow was so intent on killing him? It could have very easily killed Maradish before he even realized the intruder was in the room. Who was that shadow, and how or from where did it acquire the knowledge to defeat the security system, one of the more sophisticated in existence, and get inside his apartment WITHOUT being detected until it was ALMOST too late? Could it be another agent? Its movements were so very quiet; had it not been for the small flash of light, he would not have known it was in the apartment, and he would be dead now. Then there was that reflection; unable to distinguish whether it was a male or a female? It was ALL very puzzling and disquieting.

He was approaching the cabin, and the bike was beginning to slow for the landing on a spot less than ten feet from the door. More from a habit than anything else, he looked all around and scanned the ground for any sign of someone or anything that was not supposed to be there. Staff should not have been concerned; no one, until he broadcast the coordinates on the radio, knew he even had a cabin in the woods.

The air bike slowly descended, totally stopped in any forward motion. As he scanned the sky, he saw air cars and bikes approaching from several different directions. It had to be other agents; the code transmitted was supposed to be ultra secure and therefore only other agents SHOULD know what was said and the coordinates of the cabin.

With a soft landing, he quickly got off the bike and hurried to the door. His fingers swiftly pressed buttons of a keypad, and he said, "Exploit nine, nine, alpha nine." The door opened, and as he rushed back to get Maradish, he carried her into the cabin and placed her on the only bed in the one large room. His next stop was a panel on the wall. Here, he activated switches, and every wall suddenly turned into the scene outside the cabin. When he had the cabin built, it was built without windows; the outside was projected onto every wall and on the entire wall. This was to prevent anyone from "looking" inside, but he would be able to view all the activity of the entire area outside the cabin.

As each wall had the complete panorama of the outside, he could watch as vehicles, bikes, and cars were landing at various areas on the ground outside.   He was relieved when he saw Narvicta arrive and get out of one of the vehicles. Narvicta, the team physician, was followed closely by Taygo, the team leader.

Narvicta: Male, from the planet Eloonia, known as an Eonic, pale white, tall and slender, head physician of the team of physicians that traveled on most but not necessarily all missions. All the physicians were highly trained specialists, especially in surgery.

Taygo: lead agent on the team with Stafic, male, from the planet Kapishia, known as Kap'pi, light brown, short, and very stocky in build, able to lift twice his own body weight, but with nibble fingers and excellent eyesight, loves to work with miniatures, with a special attraction toward miniature explosives. In addition, his species was able to adjust its body to nearly twice its normal height.

Narvicta was the first to the door, and as he came in, he was asking, "What is the reason for wanting a physician?"   His primary work was surgery; he was concerned about security but was more interested in the medical needs of the Organization. His team could be in jeopardy if there was a breach.

Upon explaining all he knew of the situation, Narvicta decided perhaps it would be best to give Maradish a short examination. Stafic turned toward the front of the house to watch other air vehicles arriving; there must be more than a dozen scattered over the front yard. Out of the corner of his eye, he saw Narvicta pass a small wand attached with a thin wire to a small box over Maradish, beginning with her abdomen and stopping at the top of her head. Narvicta turned toward Stafic and said, "I believe I found the problem. There appears to be a small foreign object located between her eyes and near the top of her nose. I am not for sure, but it could be the device that is causing her the pain."

"Can it be removed?" asks Stafic.

"It will be a very delicate operation. If it is there to control her, there is a distinct possibility that it may have a small explosive device as well, and any attempt to remove it may cause it to explode and kill her instantly." Stafic looked around the gathering crowd for some kind of comment or support. All he saw were sad faces; each knew the relationship between him and Maradish and realized it was a decision he would have to make on his own. With his heart breaking, he said reluctantly, "It must come out. Remove it."

Narvicta turned back toward Maradish, injected something into her arm, and attached a wire and an additional long tube-like device to the small box. He began to push the tube, very slowly and deliberately, into her nose. Stafic heard him say in almost a whisper, "If it doesn't work, it will be a waste of such a beautiful body." Speaking more to himself than anyone, he said under his breath, "Sure don't see what this beauty she sees in him."

The room, although large, was being filled to capacity as more agents arrived. All remained very quiet, eyes fixed on Narvicta.

With steady hands, Narvicta moved very slowly, one hand with the wand and eye on the instrument, and the other hand pushing, ever so gradually, the tube into her nostril. So slow were his movements that it seemed like hours had elapsed before he stopped. With perspiration running down his face, he began to very slowly twist the tube first one way and then the other.

In spite of the large number of individuals in the room, it was so quiet that breathing was the only sound that was heard. Each knew what was at stake, and even breathing was as shallow as possible so as not to cause any distraction.

ALL were watching intently, Narvicta with a steady hand twisted the tube until he suddenly stopped and ever so slowly began to withdraw the tube. He stopped, took a breath, looked up, and said with a very firm voice, "Everyone, get away from the fireplace! It is about to come out, and I want to try to throw it into the fireplace. I have no idea if there is or will be any type of explosion. No sense in anyone else getting hurt!"

There was a sudden shuffle of dozens of feet and the noise of several individuals quickly moving away from the fireplace. It took less than a couple of seconds to clear the area.

With the area clear, Narvicta began to slowly extract the tube. Suddenly, the tube was out! With a quick twist of the wrist, the tube with a small object attached flew across the room. The tube twisted through the air like a wiggling snake, landed on the floor short of the fireplace, made a slight bounce before exploding with a loud BANG! The explosion was not very powerful, but had it exploded inside the head of Maradish, it no doubt would have been fatal and possibly removed a large portion of her skull as well.

Narvicta sat back and wiped the perspiration from his brow. Several of the onlookers rushed to him, congratulating him on a successful operation and no one being injured. He turned back to Maradish and injected something into her arm. Then he announced, "She should be awake in about five minutes."

It was when the commotion quieted down that Taygo turned to Stafic and asked, "Wa dis abo s crur baak?" (Translated, What's this about a security breach?)

As a Kap'pi, Taygo could not pronounce certain sounds or words, especially when intermixed with guttural sounds, so for clarity, I will attempt, from this point, to translate into easier-to-understand words.

The other team leaders moved closer to learn about the supposed problem, Brukist, Zennim, and Pralliun, and the fifth, Datseric, the senior leader of the group. He had very recently returned from a mission, but left the debriefing when he heard the emergency transmission, the possible breach in security, and proceeded directly to the coordinates.

Brukist, male, medium build, very light tan, with legs stronger and longer than most, noted for being able to run very long distances and faster than many others, from the planet Diiterio, but is known as a Vappiter.

Zennim, male, short, only about four feet tall, dull grey, from the planet Ciport, known as a Popirtew, able to adjust his body to squeeze through openings one quarter his size.

Prallium, gender unknown, although the gender was unknown, it was very apparent that each had the same strength, looks, and abilities, color would change from off white to dark grey for reasons unknown to any "outsider", from Vecretew but known as a Frennio, extremely pragmatic and thoughtful.

Datseric, male, very light brown with dark, almost black eyes, from Liorpre, known as a Liorope, strong physical strength, natural leader, designated as the leader of the five.

Stafic began to recount the events up to the present and his reasoning for there had to be a breach in their security. All were listening quietly as he began and were startled by a loud shout from behind them. "What is going on here? Why all the people?"

Almost as one person, the group spun around to find Maradish standing next to the bed, hands on her hips and glaring at the group.

"Well, is ANYONE going to tell me what is going on?" She shouted.

"Sure." Said a female agent, "But don't think you should get dressed first." It was then that Maradish realized she was standing totally nude.

A roar of laughter and whistles erupted as she screamed and scrambled to find something to cover herself. She found the blanket and quickly wrapped it around herself.

Some laughter continued as she scrambled, and there were a few other comments shouted, "Don't cover." "That was beautiful!" "B E AU T I FUL!" "No sense covering, we have seen it all already!"

Several of the female agents rushed to her to assist and make sure she was covered while shouting at the males to quiet themselves and not make a big thing out of it. Stafic also pushed his way through the crowd of onlookers to assist and try to explain to her why she was in such a condition. It took a lot of persuasive talk by him and the other female agents to finally calm her down enough to explain the situation.

Others in the room listened, murmuring comments quietly until Stafic had finished relating the entire story from the beginning.

Questions began from the agents: "Who?" "Why?" "Why just you?" "Is it really some kind of conspiracy, or is someone just out to get you personally?"

Stafic replied, "I have no idea how to answer all these questions. I can only speak of what has happened and what I think. I hope I am wrong, but the evidence to me points to someone attempting to eliminate me. I have no idea why."

Then he continued, "Whoever or for whatever reason, the one I encountered had the knowledge and, what is more disturbing, the expertise to disable a sophisticated alarm system to gain access to my apartment, AND with the expertise of an agent. MY opinion is that if there is one, there may be more; if there IS more, there must be someone with knowledge of our training methods involved. My suggestion is that we ALL should be very careful. I may not be the only one being targeted, but perhaps only the first. I might add whoever it is was somehow able to work THROUGH Maradish to accomplish the task, which, to me, makes it even more unnerving."

Comments began to be shouted by other agents, "That's right, an attack on one is an attack on us all!" "Need to get to the bottom of this."

"Could it be coming from the top?" "What CAN we do?"

That was when Taygo, along with the other team leaders, called for quiet.

Datseric was the first to speak. "If I may", he began. "I just returned from a mission. I lost more of my team than usual. Of course, we all know things such as this can happen, but I will only say, sometimes it happens, BUT it almost appeared they knew we were coming, and even to the time the attack was to start. It may have been a coincidence, but coupled with the events here, as stated, it now becomes very suspicious in my mind."

Taygo then spoke, "Stafic and Maradish are part of my team. What happened is highly irregular, but before we fly into a rage and do something regrettable, more investigation is needed."

Zennin added when he said," Taygo is exactly right. Everyone, return to your places, and use every possible means to remain safe. Stay on the alert for ANYTHING unusual. The five of us will conduct a thorough investigation, and as soon as we have positive information, we will let each of you know. Let me add, it may take some time."

As all the agents began to leave, many discussing the events, Targo said, "If you please, all team leaders and top agents remain, we need to talk as soon as everyone is gone."

As the last agent left, there sat and stood around the only table in the room five team leaders and nine of the top agents of the Organization, one of whom was killed on the last raid.

Maradish began, "This is very disturbing for me, to think something like this could happen and I not be able to do a thing about it."

Staffic said, "If someone, somehow, could insert a control device in your head, it should be disturbing!   And then control you into wanting to kill me; I would say IT IS MOST DISTURBING!"

"That is absurd, I wouldn't do anything like that. It may be time for me to retire."

"I think on your own, NO! But you were under the control of someone else.   It all started after our mission to Teravoka, remember?"

"Of course I do, that was where I almost lost my arm."

"We were briefed before the mission, the people there were not to be trusted, they were prone to lie or even act if they THOUGHT it could be to their advantage."

"I remember."

"We had completed our mission, and we were withdrawing. One of them had laid his weapons down in surrender, and we lowered ours in acknowledgement. It was all over. Suddenly, he had a small weapon and fired, it was only because of his bad aim or your movement, it hit your arm, nearly ripping it off. I returned fire, and he was killed. I picked you up and carried you toward the area of the physicians and called for their exact location. The physicians began immediately to repair the wound. As soon as they informed me you would be all right, my temper boiled over, and I went back and proceeded to eliminate any and all Teravoka I saw. I must admit, I killed almost indiscriminately and may have killed too many. Once my anger had cooled, I went back to where I had left you."

"I don't remember anything after being wounded. The first thing I recall was on the flight back to Traket."

"The only time you were out of my sight was during the operation and the flight on the supply ship back to Traket. Those were the only times you were out of my sight, and the implant was to be inserted. Which means to me, whoever did the implant had to have the knowledge and time to do it. To me, it seems we are dealing with a group rather than a single individual, with the know-how to defeat security devices and KNOW our tactics and be able to perform that delicate a surgery."

Then Taryo spoke, "The problem is we do not know for sure whether there is or was only one involved, a large group or team of individuals. We do not need to condemn anyone until we KNOW who, how many, and very importantly, why? That is not the only problem; they may have access to our codes. If security systems can be compromised, we can only assume our radio codes have also been compromised.   Therefore, anything transmitted is subject to interception, and ALL our communications are done by radio."

"That is understandable. What or how can we avoid any interception?" Asked Maradish.

"We can't", said Stafic.

Taygo then said, "This is strictly between us; we will have to have some kind of code to let us know we are talking only to the ones in this room."

"That still would not avoid interception," advised Zennim. "If they know the codes, security would be nil."

"Perhaps we should begin any transmission with a code word, "zebra four and the name to receive the message, and end with three four," suggested Pralliun. "It would mean we will have to monitor each other's frequency." (Translated "zebra four" means a private call, and three four is the same as ten four in police communications on earth, message sent and no reply necessary.) "Perhaps, using that and a different code system?" Said Brukist, thoughtfully.

"We could use a private courier," Suggested Huttified, one of the top agents.

"That would require time to get a message to everyone and time we may not have." Said Datseric.

"There must be a better and faster way," said Stafic.

"I read about something called teletype that was used a long time ago, it required, I think, something called a keyboard and wires, it was very private, one-to-one communication," Said Struffpoic, another top agent with a hobby in ancient history. "But that was generations ago."

"I think I know how to solve our problem," said Brukist. "Adjust our spare radio to a series of frequencies, let's say eight. When transmitting a message, the radio would only remain on a single frequency for, let's say, three seconds before changing to another. The frequencies could be set in the same arbitrary frequencies and changed if needed or on a set timetable. Any interception would only hear a single word or two, but our radios would receive the message uninterrupted."

"Can that be done?" Ask Taygo.

"I worked in communications before becoming a team leader, and yes, with some adjustments."

"Sounds like the remedy,"

"Sounds good."

"Perfect solution," said almost everyone at the same time. "I'll send a courier to gather all the radios as quietly as possible. The only problem will be with fifteen radios to adjust; it may take a week or longer to get them all synchronized."

"Very good." Said Datseric. "I'll have to let you know who my second top agent will be."

With that problem seemingly solved, the group dispersed to their various homes, and the two, Maradish and Stafic, were left alone to ponder all that had transpired. Alone, the two again reviewed the circumstances since the mission to Teravoka. Quietly prepared and ate their meal; it had been a long day, and both retired to bed for a night of restless sleep.

II

It was almost two weeks later when Stafics' primary radio crackled with the a message which sounded just like Taygo with the sound of his voice but did not say the code words nor was it on his secondary radio. Stafic and Maradish listened carefully and as they translated the code words, it was very apparent to them it was NOT Taygo. The information transmitted according to the codes indicated Taygo had information and was to meet with Stafic at an inn and the coordinates indicated the location to be about a hundred thirty miles away.

"It is a trap", stated Maradish flatly.

"I fully agree, whoever is setting it wants me to spring it. I really have no choice." Stafic acknowledged the transmission and gave the estimate of arrival which would be late in the day and they could meet on the day after to advise of a good time to meet. The next transmission indicated Stafic was to meet with an Issitaric, Twiccyan by name and a time would be given when he arrived. This to him and Maradish was just another red flag, why would Taygo want to meet with him with information and THEN he was to send someone else with the information and why not issue the time right away. Perhaps this may the first mistake of whoever is behind this problem.

Issitarics were easily identifiable, tall, normally over seven feet, and covered with red hair. Not known to be very aggressive, very calm and peaceful and not prone to engage in any type of violate behavior. Used very often by the Empire as a negotiator, especially in delicate matters of peace or trade. To Stafic, it meant, a Issitaric was somehow convinced to be a part of the trap or someone only disguised as one to make it easy to identify and keep him relaxed. The Issitaric it seems was to alleviate any sense of apprehension. In either case, in only provided another reason this was meant to be a one way trip for him therefore extra precautions would be needed.

Stafic spoke to his computer and repeated the coordinate and said, "I want a detailed map of the area, out to twenty miles and the floor plan of the inn."

"Do you HAVE to go?" Pleaded Maradish.

"Its either go and be aware of what I am stepping into or wait for them to make a move at their convenience. Taygo must have received the same message, so call him on the secondary radio and check while I pack and get ready."

" Taygo said he heard everything and to be extra careful;" As Stafic prepared to leave, Maradish ask. "Why are you getting ready now? The meeting time is not for the day after tomorrow."

"I will stay overnight at the Inn, whoever is behind all this, I hope, will not be expecting me to arrive today maybe throw them off balance. I figure, if they are able to do what they have already, anything I can do the keep them a step behind or off balance, I need to do."

"Of course your right, I would do the same but I thought maybe we could have some time alone."

"THAT does sound great, maybe an hour or so. But unless this is cleared we may never have any more time alone again."

He proceeded to pack his weapons and uniform clothes as if he was leaving for another mission and an experimental set of armor the scientist wanted him to try out for wear ability on his next mission. All agents wore armor on their missions, it was little protection for a close range with a full power blast but offered some protection for many of the other encounters, the Organization scientists were hoping this would be better.

Stafic and Maradish spent a couple of hours together, ate a quiet meal before Stafic said tenderly, "While I am gone, buy some clothes and anything else you need. Charge it to my account, I'll see you in a few days."

Stafic would use the air bike and leave the air car he had stored at the cabin and had used for his long excursions; for Maradish. He dressed as a tourist and then loaded the luggage on the air bike, set the coordinates for the inn, speed on normal and was ready to go. With a kiss and a hug from

Maradish, he was on the bike, started the engine and roared off into the air. At normal speed, he would approach the inn in about three hours.   About thirty minutes from the inn he would reduce to a much slower speed.

With speed and the avoidance system activated, Stafic relaxed to study the information given him about the Inn and surrounding area. The first thing he noticed was where the inn was located, in a valley surrounded on three sides by hills. There was basically only one way to enter the inn and appeared there was no back entrance. Surrounded by heavy woods with only a single entry cut through the woods, it faced a lake and a boat dock. He thought to himself, "An ideal setup for an ambush, only one structured way into the area, unless you arrive over the lake or over or through the mountains somehow. With a single way in they would have only the one way to watch for his arrival." Nothing he could do about it so he relaxed for the duration on the trip and his thoughts began to try to determine some way of keeping the opponent off balance, he wanted to do something not expected, but what? What if they DID expect him to arrive early? They were very familiar with his methods and actions?? If they determined he would arrive early, there is the possibility they could be waiting for him. What a terrible thought, he might be by arriving early and allow them to spring the trap, EARLY!

As he approached, about thirty minutes from the inn, Stafic adjusted the computer to assume manual control. He reduced speed to nearly a third of the previous speed.   Scanned the map once more, turned off the structured entry to the inn, and went to a hill from which he could observe a large portion of the valley below. The inn was among the thick trees and the trees extending down to the lake, the only clear areas was the structured entry and the area in front of the inn which extended down to the lake for access to the boat houses and ramp. The inn appeared to be about a thousand feet from the lake and the boat dock which had several associated buildings.

From the top of the hill, he observed the activity in the valley below through his binoculars. He watched as individuals entered and left the area, the watercrafts on the lake and generally everyone appeared to be relaxing and enjoying themselves. Even dressed as a tourist he knew he would be easily recognized, it would have been difficult even if he wanted to cover all of his blue skin. As soon as he checked in, he was sure those of which he came to see would know he was there. His intention was to maybe cause them to wonder why he arrived a day sooner.

Back on his bike, he proceeded on to the inn. Upon arriving, he made it no secret he was there, as much as possible, making enough noise to be noticed but not so much to be irritating. At the check in counter, he requested a room, given a room on the second floor and walked casually up the stairs and to the room. To most, he appeared to be just another tourist, come to relax and enjoy the quiet surroundings, maybe a boat trip or fishing trip on the lake. Few paid any attention or it appeared not to pay any attention to the individual with blue skin or even later as he sat at his supper meal that evening.

The next morning as he sat eating his breakfast, he had thoughts of the days when as a teenager when he and his family sat at their meal. He had not thought of those days since becoming an agent for the "Organization". He had not had the time nor the opportunity. The food was good but he never quite got use to the taste, it was different from the food he had grown use to in his growing years. Suddenly his thoughts were interrupted by the voice of the serving robot. "Mister Tiqup'p-Tkeromivver'p't, sir, there is a message for you."

"Yes. What is it?"

"Meet me at the boat dock for private meeting, eight o'clock."

"Thank you!"

"Any return message?"

"NO. Thank You." Then he thought, "They know for sure he was here and most likely knew he had arrived yesterday." He casually finished his meal and returned to his room. He wondered as he walked back to his room, "Why they didn't attempt to kill him as he wandered around the inn yesterday. Maybe to many witnesses? The message DID say private!"

Relaxing in the room, his next thing to determine was what they expected him to do. They knew his capabilities apparently enough not to try anything to which he would have the advantage, like in this room. So what could he do to throw them off balance. One thing; they would expect him to use his stealth ability, maybe leave the room after dark via a window and sneak through the trees to the rendezvous point, the meeting WAS for eight and it would be dark. He knew now what he would do, they, whoever they are, would not expect his next move however once in motion, the problem would to keep them guessing to what he would do next. THAT would be the biggest problem and still stay alive to tell about it.

As the evening approached, Stafic began to prepare for the encounter. Instead of dressing in the clothing suitable for a stealth maneuver, he dressed for a face to face encounter. He had packed for both before leaving Maradish. As he put on the armor, he knew it was experimental. They told him they hoped it would be capable of absorbing part if not all the energy from a weapon, but perhaps not the force of the energy. This would be the first test with an individual directly involved. The scientist needed to know if how the armor actually performs, its' comfortable level, any movement deficiencies or any other problems. They did not know it would be "tested" this quickly.

With each piece of the equipment firmly in place, it would now only be less than forty five minutes to the make or break point. The body armor was complete with chest, leg and partial arm protection down to the elbow. With his helmet with shatter proof glasses and the uniform, he was slightly uncomfortable. He appeared to be government military soldier on a combat mission instead of an agent for the "Organization". Armed with a long range weapon, two shorter range hand weapons, stun grenades and several other weapons, he walked out of the room and down the stairs and straight to the check-in desk.

To the individual behind the desk he said, "This is an emergency! Announce to everyone to go to their rooms, find cover and remain as far away as possible from the front of the inn. There may be weapons discharged and I do NOT want anyone to be injured or possibly killed. Keep all the lights on full intensity."

The clerk starred at the individual across the desk, said "YES SIR!" Then with a microphone in hand announced, "Emergency! Emergency! THIS IS AN EMERGENCY! All guests proceed immediately to your assigned rooms or take cover! All employees and guests take immediate cover! Emergency! Emergency! Everyone clear the lobby and remain completely clear of the entrance doors until further advised!" The message was repeated two more times.

There was a sudden rush of individuals running to the rooms with their mates and off springs. In a matter of what seemed seconds the lobby was clear of guests and perhaps seconds later the employees were running for cover for anything they hoped would be some kind of protection. Only the server robots remained in the open with only knowledge of the sudden disappearance of the guests and with no one to serve just stopped and remained still.

Stafic began to walk toward the entrance. With deliberate and steady steps, He reached the entrance in just a few seconds. As he walked toward the large doors, he thought of activating his infra-red sensors and shield but realized they would be useless with all the bright lights and heat from them. He pushed through the doors, he had enough time to walk to the boat dock and be there almost exactly at eight .   A couple more steps and he was outside and in the cool night air. He watched as a few stragglers as they rushed away from the area and toward protection or to their rooms. He thought any one or more of these could be part of his welcoming committee.

As his eyes adjusted to the light, in the distance was a silhouette of someone standing on the deck, outside one of the buildings. The lights of the building had been dimmed so that the figure, could be barely be identified to be an Issitaric without very much detail. It appeared to be standing alone, arms at its sides and no weapon in view. Of course, not being able not to see a weapon would not mean there was not one readily available or even if the figure was actually alone for that matter, the deck was constructed in a way that the lower part of the individual was not visible.

The building appeared a plain and simple building with windows on the side, a deck of some kind along its entire length and a guard rail extending up to about the waist high to the standing figure. If it was an

Issitaric, it would indicate the guard rail would be about three to three and half feet in height.

The stage was set, Stafic began to walk, he was in the open, anyone with any kind of ability to fire a weapon, if among the trees could easily fire at him, unseen, until it was too late to react. The only advantage was, they did not know he would be walking boldly out the front entrance, perhaps would be on watch in a different direction and maybe need to move to get in position to shoot. It may just be enough movement for him to react, at least that was his hope.

Almost half way to the figure, he was still standing very still; Stafic would soon be within the lethal range of any know weapon of which he had knowledge. His muscles began to tense, at the first indication of movement or sound of a voice, he would have to react relying upon his quick reflexes. The normal reaction for him would be to jump or move to his right, he would have to concentrate on a different direction or motion. He had to assume they knew how he normally would react.

Suddenly, with a quick move, the figure dove to one side exposing a window behind it. From the window a blue streak flashed striking Stafic in the chest. The armor absorbed the deadly energy but the force knocked him backward. As he stumbled backward, he already had his weapon in hand and fired at the figure. His shot hit the guard rail, ripping a hole through it. Before he could squeeze another shot, flashes of blue energy erupted from the trees on both sides. None the energy being expended appeared to be hitting anywhere around or even near his person.

He staggered backward from the hit in the chest, he caught himself enough to move quickly to the left. With the quick move to his left, he fired his second shot at the window. It hit the window, but an instant before it hit, a second shot flashed from the window, it hit him in the leg, the force knocking his leg from under him, spinning him around and he fell to the ground, more blue energy beams came from the trees hitting the window, from the window there were no more shots fired. The other figure raised up to shoot, several streaks of energy from the trees on both sides, they hit at the same time, this figure was instantly vaporized.

Though on the ground, a movement was seen in the trees, he swung his weapon to engage when a voice shouted, "STAFIC! Don't shoot ! It's Mjonic and Traviper."   Stafic lowered his weapon as two of the team members emerged from the trees on his right and two more emerged from the trees on the left.

"You didn't think we were going to let you have all the fun did you?"

"Taygo sent us and said he would have been here except he thought he might be recognized."

"You must be a very dangerous person! They had three on both side waiting in ambush for you."

The four team members as they emerged into the open area were laughing and all trying to talk at the same time but that was when Mjonic saw the burned hole in the leg of the uniform of Stafic. "What happened there? And there?" pointing to his leg.

"Small problem, the armor worked but it sure got hot for a moment. Really need to get out of it."

"Well", Stafic continued. "I will tell you each one I am sure glad you were here. I thought for a moment when I got hit it was all over."

Traviper said, "Hurrijuw and I were here when you arrived last evening, Mjonic and Pavtiton came in early this morning. We were all in position since about noon, even watched the others take their places for your ambush."

"I tried to surprise them by coming out the front doors," said Stafic.

"You surprised us for sure," mentioned Pavtiton.

"Yeah! Nearly caught us off guard too," the other said in unison.

"It is unfortunate the Issitaric could not have been taken alive," said Mjonic sadly. "It may have had some important information."

"No sense thinking what might have been," Hurrijuw said pragmatically.

"The others were and he was; what is called "expendable", they know nothing except to follow orders. If they get killed it is just to bad, there is always more where they came from," said Traviper.

"That is sad but true," Stafic nearly whispered.

"Least we were never considered expendable, to much has been invested in our training. In fact the Organization has gone to great lengths to provide protection. Just look at the holes in the uniform of Stafic," said Mjonic proudly.

"How true! That is what makes this problem so unlike the powers of the Organization," said Stafic.

"Yeah! If they don't need us anymore why not just give us all a retirement so we can go back to our own places in peace," said Pavtiton, beginning to be angry about the entire situation.

"Perhaps! They feel we may reassemble, so the best way to prevent that is to do what we are hired to do; destroy the organization from the top down," mentioned Hurrijuw thoughtfully.

"IF YOUR RIGHT!" Traviper nearly shouted. "All our leaders and top agents are targets, we ALL better be on special lookout because it is FAR from being over," said Traviper.

Then Stafic said, "Use the secondary radio and advise Taygo there is a need for us to meet all together. The ones we are dealing with are pros;

that one in the window was a trained shooter as you can witness to the hit I took in the chest and the leg. I think we are dealing with a very powerful individual or group. Let me know what he says as I get out of these clothes, they are not the most comfortable."

"We can fully agree on that! That hit was exactly on target," said Mjonic as he placed his fingers into the burnt material. "That armor seems to have saved your life!"

"And my leg," added Stafic.

The five had always been brothers on missions but have now become even closer brothers in arms. They began laughing and talking again as they attempted to put it all out their mind and proceeded back to the Inn with the confidence they were truly more than just members of a team.

Stafic made a quick call to Maradish to inform her all was OK and he would be returning home the next morning. After resting and a morning meal, all five would leave the Inn, wondering what would be next, whoever was behind this, what might be the next move. Each of them had to keep on a special alert, whomever was behind all this has become even more dangerous and maybe even unpredictable because it was now known that every member of the team will come to the aid of the others and there was still no way to tell from where the power might be originating.

III

It was three weeks later radio message addressed to Stafic from Taygo was received. It was in code; alpha ninety four A 75 36 22 47 zema mike 6. Translated it said a meeting for the team leaders and Stafic ONLY to attend at coordinates 75 36-22 44 and the meeting to take place in three days.   This fact raised the suspicion in their minds because although when conversing over the radio and a specific person was mentioned, another private meeting was mentioned.   The reason and the agreed beginning and ending of the message was Not given.   In fact, the last conversation, Taygo made a point that communication from him would always be for both of them. The opponent must realize that the radio was being monitored and any number of agents would become involved thus the reason for strictly private for Stafic only and maybe the others would ignore it, after all it was, supposedly from Taygo.

Stafic using gestures they often used on a mission when quiet was necessary, gestured to Maradish to not say a word, he said, "It appears Taygo wants some kind of information only I can give him or maybe some kind of personal information I need.   If it is either one, before I go, lets you and I have some quiet time together. You know something I would like, a picnic, I have not been on a picnic since, well since I can't remember the last time."

"That is a GREAT idea, it has been years for me as well."

Stafic walked to the fireplace, removed a brick and turned on a switch.

"I activated a sound suppressor, it created the normal sounds of someone moving about the cabin, even a conversation between the two of them. Just a precaution, I guess, in case there was some listening device capable of hearing our conversation. For some reason you are again being excluded from this", began Stafic. "This is another reason you must the center of this and they, whoever they are, want you to stay out of harms way." He paused, then continued, "Taygo, I know heard but I don't know if he will be personally involved. If not, I on my way and will have to expect most anything. No matter what happens, there MUST be a solution, the future of the Organization is at stake not to mention the lives and livelihood of the rest of the agents."

"You are sounding like you may not return from this one," said Maradish nearly in tears.

"You know that is ALWAYS a possibility on any mission but there is even more of the possibility for this one. We are dealing with someone who knows how and the way we work as well as we do."

"Then I don't want you to go," tears now flowing from her black eyes.

"Please. You know I must, otherwise, there will be no rest for any of us plus there is no telling what our opponent may do next. Now lets go on a picnic."

"I know but I still don't want you to go. Please be careful and come back to me."

Stafic reached to the switch and turned it off. With the switch deactivated, the two of them put together a picnic lunch and left for a park a few miles away.

It was late in the morning of the second day, Maradish activated the sound suppressor and announced, "When you come back, you will find me at my farm, absolutely no one knows these coordinates; 22-58, 41-0

here is the list of the codes for each of ten security devises, the house is protected with a force field, the last code will allow access. You need to leave your bike in the shelter and walk the pathway to the house, deactivate the devises along the way. When she finished speaking she reactivated to the normal sounds of the house.

Reluctantly everything was packed and they began packing the air bike for the trip to almost the other side of the planet. They packed as if Stafic was leaving for a mission for the Organization, complete with weapons, offensive and defensive, armor and everything available as if going on a mission. Neither said much as they packed, the prospects of a successful return weighed heavy on their minds.

The air bike was finally packed and Stafic sadly said, "There that is the last of everything" and holding his fingers to his lips for silence said,

"The meeting may take a couple of days, a day back, I should see you in about three or four days from now."

"You can tell me all about it and why I couldn't attend when you get back", Maradish returned going along with the possibility of being heard by the opposition.

"I am sure there MUST be a reason, see you then." Stafic then climbed on the bike, set the computer, threw Maradish a kiss and roared off toward the rendezvous. Maradish was left standing at the door of the cabin, a very sad look on her face, waving with a very weak and slow hand.

IV

Stafic set the controls on automatic with the avoidance system activated. The bike would carry him to the proper coordinates at a speed slightly more than normal. At normal speed it would have taken him more than a day, the destination was only a rest stop normally only a single building for travelers leaving the city and traveling to recreation areas on the other side of the planet. At this speed he would arrive about two hours after sunrise and about seven to eight hours before the scheduled time of the supposed meeting. All he had to do now was relax, rest as much as possible.

With time to think, his first thought was why a rest stop, a single building in the middle of a wide expanse of open land. There should be a number of travelers there, most if not all in and around the building, there was very little to do except stretch your legs wait for to board the transit for the next leg of the journey.

He began to wonder exactly what the opponent could have in mind, it was difficult to determine when there was no idea who or even what kind of species you were dealing with. If it were known, there was an action which could be anticipated but..... To risk an open confrontation would put an unknown number of individuals jeopardy, unless THAT WAS the intention. With the knowledge of the agents and even the inner workings of the organization, the reluctance to place innocents in the line of fire it may be the exact place to do what they deem necessary?

He approached the coordinates, he disengaged the automatic flight controls and turned off course. He found a hilltop from which he could observe the activity below without being observed. He realized there was a strong possibility the opponent also would realize that is exactly what he would do also. It had now become a "cat and mouse" game. Were they expecting him to do something out of character or something he normally would do?

As he looked over the area he thought to himself, "whoever it is could be out of sight among the wooded area or could be any one or number of the individuals, disguised, as tourists below. His only way to find out is to be a tourist also." He saw nothing unusual or of any significance to attract his attention. He decided to try to make "them" believe he was arriving on the next transit as a tourist. But exactly how he wasn't sure.

Deep in thought , he literally jumped when his radio suddenly crackled to life. "Stafic, Taygo, have arrived, awaiting your arrival, say E.T.A." (Estimated time of arrival). The transmission sounded exactly like Taygo, the code was not mentioned BUT maybe not necessarily needed, if it were just he and himself on the other side of the planet.? He was actually less than five minutes away but said, "E.T.A. twenty minutes." Observing the activity below he thought another transit was approaching therefore just thought of a number. He purposely did not mention any of the preplanned codes so Taygo, or if anyone else was listening, both would be receiving the same information. Stafic would just have to hope that the real Taygo, if he was around, would know the E.T.A. was false.

The next problem was to arrive in the area as undetectable as possible and still be able to see from if there was any way of detecting who, where and how many opponents were involved. He decided to, because he was dressed the part, arrive dressed as a tourist but underneath would wear his armor. This would exposed his bluish skin but they knew he was arriving very soon so there was no need to try to hide the fact. He quickly undressed and redressed, it left exposed his arms and head but that would have to be the way it would have to be.

As he was about to mount back on his bike, his radio once more crackled to life. "Stafic, Taygo, meet me in the restaurant, table far left and back." That is when Stafic thought about the arriving transit.

"Roger Taygo, arriving on next transit, will see you then," replied Stafic. He realized this message would tell Taygo he had issued a false arrival time. Taygo would never give his exact location especially when he knew his adversary was listening to every transmission. For whatever reason, the false Taygo wanted him in the restaurant. He thought it would be best to remain out of the way but close enough to see what will transpire.

From his vantage point, Stafic watched as one transit loaded, departed and another arrived and began to discharge its passengers.

"What is your location now?" Came the voice over the radio.

"Just leaving the transit and will enter the restaurant very shortly," Stafic replied. He was curious as to why it was important to know exactly where he was, but said nothing.

"Advise when inside the restaurant."

"Will do, last one off the transit". Stafic was attempting to delay as much as possible in hopes of the opponents would expose themselves, he realized he was NOT talking to Taygo, Taygo would never keep asking where he was, he would have just waited for him to arrive, he had already given where to find him. What was this interest in KNOWING his exact location?

More curious than anything else, Stafic said, "Stepping through the door now."

The words were scarcely out of his mouth when there was an explosion of such force it knocked Stafic off his feet. Debris of all kinds was flying overhead and raining down on him.

"WHAT was that?" was the first impulsive thought, then he realized what must have happened. He quickly got to his feet, tried as best he could to protect himself from falling debris and looked down toward the place where a building use to be. There was nothing there except a huge crater. The explosion had obliterated the building, the parking area and part of the surrounding tree line, knocking over many trees beyond and the individuals who had not gone into the restaurant all around apparently dead or had disappeared. There were scattered fires all around, any bodies or parts of bodies as well bits, pieces and parts of the building were still falling back into the crater burning.   The crater appeared to be over a hundred yards across. It was a scene of nearly complete devastation. No one could have possibly survived.

Stafic looked at the devastation, he became sick, the loss of all those lives, individuals who were only going somewhere for a "vacation", to relax and have some fun but happened to be in the wrong place at the wrong moment. Whoever the opponent was, there was no regard or even thought of sacrificing innocents to accomplish whatever it was trying to accomplish. It was not like he had never seen or even participated in the death of others, they were combatants, and it was a military operation. These were innocents; no battle was raging, there was no combatants engaged and innocents happened to get in the way. Stafic, then became very angry, his temper flared but there was no one upon of whom he could exact his anger, least no one he could see. Even the Acfitrerric, who have little regard for life except their own, would have never extracted this much and type of carnage on purely innocent people.

As his temper cooled, he thought there was nothing to be done here, better get back to Maradish, then another thought occurred, whoever it was, must now believe he and Taygo were dead. He would return in a long, round about way to make sure he was unobserved as much as possible which meant he would not be able to use his radio even to let her know of he was ok, he was on his way back or even where he was at the present time. Thinking, if the explosion was from the adversary, it must have been done by remote that was why the questions about where he was right up to the explosion. He or she may still be in the area. He would need start by the physically move of his bike to a place where the start of the engine would not be heard, in case there was anyone around that may hear and hopefully pay little attention, once started the engine is be nearly soundless.

As he pushed the bike, the thought occurred if the explosion was detonated by remote, the adversary could be no where around but he could not take that chance.   Or maybe the explosion was more powerful than anticipated and the perpetrator also died in the blast. The last thought made him smile, would serve him right to die with all the others. Considered a safe distance, he started the engine which roared to life like a hungry tsrufical. (A lion type animal the size of an elephant.)

On his bike, he headed not toward the coordinates given to him by Maradish but in a direction almost away from them. Precaution was foremost on his mind, he HAD to be sure no one knew he was still alive, it would mean arriving at the farm after dark. With the avoidance system set on maximum, he would remain just above the tree tops at a speed below normal cruise.

V

It was late and dark when Stafic arrived at the pathway entrance to the farmhouse. To his surprise, his detector indicated the first security devise was not activated. Not alarmed, he dismounted his bike, placed it in an area hidden from view and away from the shelter provided Maradish had mentioned and started by foot toward the house, the pathway would make several turns before reaching the house. With a hand held detector and codes he began to walk. As soon as his detector sensed a devise, he would enter the code to deactivate.

He began to walk the path but there was no indication of any security devise. At first, he was not concerned, perhaps there was a malfunction or for some reason one or two may have not been activated. He should start to encounter at least a couple devises but the farther he walked, the more he began to realize there was something very wrong, he should have encountered at least four, NONE were activated. The further he walked the more concerned and apprehensive he became, still no indication of any devises activated and THAT was not at all like Maradish. She would not purposely leave them off or forget to turn them on; something else was very wrong.. With each step, he became more apprehensive, something WAS very wrong but what? He began to walk more slowly, measuring each step. Without realizing, he had automatically entered into his stealth mode. All his training and experience bubbled to the surface, caution had kept him safe all these years. He had an immense urge to throw it all to the wind and rush toward the house a see what was wrong. He came to a turn and as he eased around the turn, the house suddenly came into view, the hair on his neck began to bristle. He immediately stopped, there HAD to be something drastically wrong! The force field, she was very particular to tell him about was NOT activated!   The house itself was dark except for one small light.

His concern for Maradish almost caused him to rush into the house and find out what was the problem, however with great effort and all the years of experience prevented him from doing exactly that. It might place her and himself in a fatal position and would help no one but the adversary, if indeed the adversary was present. Once more in full control, he began the slow and meticulous task of finding a way into the house undetected and if necessary, eliminate the opposition without bringing harm to Maradish or himself. The advantage he had was, IF there were an unknown in the house that individual would not be expecting him, he was dead.

Stafic stood quietly in the shadow, attempting to analyze the problem, it was for sure he did not know if the was another access to the inside available, he did not have his tools available to open any locked windows, unsure of a back door and if there was whether it might be locked and last, even he did gain access, not familiar with the floor plan which might hinder any movement. He decided he would attempt a frontal entry, carefully checking everyplace he could before making any step. He knew his stealth capability, to be able to get very close before being detected, he did not have the ability of Maradish but maybe he had enough.

The farmhouse was of an old fashioned design, made of lumber and plastered outside walls. With a porch which was completely across the front and on the porch were various types of chairs and sofas all in keeping with the old design of the house itself. The single light barely visible from the outside, was of little help. As he made his way onto the porch from the side and he would have to crawl slowly past each obstacle and try not to even bump against any one of them. Any sound may disclose his position. It made to movement very slow but necessary not to make any noise. He came to a window, he wished he had his periscope to look around the corner, he didn't so he activated his infra-red sensor and cautiously raised himself enough to be able to look with only one eye. There was nothing but darkness, no light, nothing he could see, no movement, it appeared to be a room. The window was closed but he tried anyway to see if it might be unlocked, it was locked, without the tool to unlock, he had to proceed to the next window.

He slowly made his way to the next window. As he peered into the window, he could see Maradish. She was sitting in a chair with her back toward the door, bent over and very still. If she was breathing, it was not noticeable to him. Suddenly, his temper began to rise, his thoughts raced, "If they had done ANY harm to her, he would not hesitate to, by himself, avenge anybody that got in his way." Once more, for the second time this day, he HAD stop to regain his composure, still in the state of anger, he HAD to control it and find if there was anyone other than Maradish in the house, what they did to her and THEN he would vent his anger.

He scanned with one eye the room she was sitting, it appeared to be a large living area, there were several doors, all appeared to be closed, closing off the room. The door leading to the outside was between the window where he was and another window on the other side. From his this point he could see most of the room but not all of it. She was sitting in a chair with a small light on what appeared to be a table next to her and other pieces of furniture neatly placed around the room but the part of the room closes to him was not totally visible. To get a better look at the room hidden for his present position, he crawled to the other window and peered in. Everything was the same except the area not visible from the other position was now visible, nothing appeared out of place or unusual and no one else visible.

Next was the door, he slowly opened the door, it was unlocked. He opened it only wide enough for him to slip through the opening and lay flat as possible on the floor next to the wall. It was then he realized, if someone else was in the house, the only weapon he had on his person was his Kafari, he had not anticipated needing any type of weapon. He lay very quiet as he scanned the entire room, there appeared to be no one but Maradish.

Rising slowly to his feet, one slow step at a time, still with caution in case there was anyone else in the house, he stepped closer and closer to

Maradish continuing to scan the room for any type of movement. Within arms reach of her, he could see she was very softly sobbing, his heart was breaking to see her cry, her kind would never allow this type of emotion in private or otherwise. Unable to stand it any longer and nearly close enough to touch her; he asked softly, "Mara, what is wrong?"

She screamed a most blood curdling scream he had ever heard, she was up from the chair, table, chair and light flying across the room. She turned to face him, still screaming something about a ghost, staggering backward, eyes wide open and even in the dull light, he could see the sheer panic in her face. Her face turned an ash grey color. Still screaming, she staggered back only a few steps before she collapsed to the floor. She had fainted. He had never seen this reaction from her, normally she should have attacked, he stood motionless for a few seconds, almost in a state of shock, before rushing to her with thoughts what could have happened, what did he do? Perhaps something occurred to her he didn't know about, did I kill my love?

He was on the floor next to her, raised her up to cradle her in his arms, not sure what to do next but could tell she at least was breathing although shallow and labored. "Mara, Mara," he called to her. "Wake up , sweet, wake up!"

What seemed like an eternity to him she began to stir, Slowly opened her eyes , looked at him, almost in a whisper, "Noooo, Ghooost," went limp and passed out once more.

Stafic thought, "She thinks I am a ghost." Suddenly he remembered, although she was from one of the most fierce species in the Empire, all of them had an intense fear of ghosts or spirits of any kind. When she began to recover again, he had to somehow convince her he was not a ghost, but why would she think he was a ghost?

As she began to recover again, he began to stroke her hair and softly say, "Mara, it is me I am not a ghost. I am real. Mara wake up. I AM alive! It's me, Stafic."

Her eyes fluttered and slowly opened, "Is it really you?' She said with a weak and trembling voice. "Is it you or is only a dream? You're not dead, not a ghost to come a haunt me?"

"It's really me, STAFIC! Would a ghost kiss you?" He kissed her with a most passionate kiss.

"You…you ..are.. not ..dead. Not a ghost." she whimpered softly.

"Definitely not a ghost and who told you I was dead?"

"I was told there was nothing even left to bury, not even a scrape of cloth." Her voice was still very weak and trembling as if she still did not believe she was talking to anything other than a ghost.

"Mara, Mara! Snap out of it. I am really here . I am not a ghost or spirit of any kind! Mara, it's me!" He nearly shouted.

"Kiss me if you're not a ghost," she replied with a weak voice.

He leaned over and a kissed her, "See, could a ghost kiss you?"

"IT IS really you! You come back to me! Kiss me again, I want you to kiss me again!"

He kissed her again.

As he withdrew from the kiss, she grabbed him around his neck and pulled him down squealing in his ears, "It is YOU! You came back! You came back to me! I love You."

He finally pulled himself loose and sat down beside her, her color was slowly returning, she was beginning to look like his Maradish again.

They sat looking at each other. Her color had returned and her breathing was normal before he ask, "Who told you I was dead?"

"It came over the radio sounded like the dispatcher, it said you and Taygo were killed. Some kind of freak accident."

"That is strange, if Taygo was in the vicinity of the explosion, maybe, but I don't believe he was, it was not anything even close to be like a freak accident. It was very deliberate. I think it may have been set off by way of remote control. What time was it when you were notified of the "accident?"

"I don't know, maybe, about ten or eleven o'clock. How do you know for certain Taygo was not there? And why deliberate? "

"He did not give the proper code words, the problem is IF he was where he said he was, which I doubt, he is dead but I believe he was giving false information the same as I was. Deliberate because of how it it occurred. The moment I said I was in the building the explosion occurred. With no survivors, who will know the difference. This is very important, think what time was it?"

"Well let's just call Taygo and find out and tell him you are still alive, he must have been told you were dead. It must have been closer to ten, I had just finished cleaning the kitchen after breakfast. Why?" "You were notified within only a couple of hours, there is no way without any communications available that could be known, the explosion leveled everything within a hundred yards. No don't call him, we finally have an advantage, no one other than you and I, I hope, Zefunia, knows we are still alive. I am sure if he is alive he has somehow let her know. IT HAS to be some high up in the government and I am also sure the radio is being closely monitored. I want you to continue in a state of mourning."

"That will be difficult for me to do, now."

"You will MUST! It is the only advantage we have at present. If you don't they will try again and next time may be successful."

"Since you put it THAT way, I'll need to do a lot of acting."

"You bet! If we are to get to bottom of this we'll need every advantage we can muster. It will HAVE to be very convincing, the best act you have ever done.   Call his wife, Zefunia, make some kind of arrangements to see her, make some kind of excuse, you know their species and how they react about a death; maybe to help with the festivities or something."

They both got up and began to walk arm in arm, "I sure am hungry", Stafic was saying. "What is there to eat?"

Stafic thought she would take him toward the kitchen but Maradish was leading him gently toward the bedroom. "I have something else in mind FIRST, then, we'll have something to eat."

"OK, I've been gaining to much weight anyway."

Later as they were sitting at the table thoughtfully thinking about everything which has happened, Stafic looked at Maradish and said, "As much as I would like to stay here, I am going to have to disappear and you are going to have think and talk as if you had never seen me and that you firmly believe the report, I am dead. The sooner I disappear the better for you and me."

"Where will you go?"

"That my sweet, you had better not know for more than several reasons. I will keep in touch, somehow."

"You COULD stay in one of the rooms here, none would know but me."

"That sounds very tempting but one miss said word and all the advantage would be for nothing."

"I would never say a word."

"I believe it but they, whoever they are, that is the problem, we have no idea who they are, may see in you an action or even a look on your face. No, as much as I would like to stay , I need to disappear for a while."

The meal complete, they went back toward the front of the house, "I don't have anything here to pack and the bike is packed so I am going to say, I love you and we will be together again once this is over, it may take longer than either of us want but it is what needs to be done." The sadness in his voice and they were parting AGAIN, brought unusual tears to the eyes of Maradish. Stafic wiped the tears away, kissed her and hurried away not wanting her to see it was breaking his heart as well and disappeared.

VI

Maradish attempted to sleep that night but was so restless she grateful when the morning arrived. She finally got up fixed her a breakfast, sat down and only looked at it, pushed it aside, she had lost her appetite . A restful sleep appeared tobe out of the question and now she was not the least bit hungry. She should be happy her Stafic was alive. He was alive, but not with her, he had been gone less than a day and she missed him already. She thought she had totally lost him once, he came back, now he is gone again. Her acting may not be as difficult as she first thought. She walked aimlessly around the farmhouse until late that morning when she decided to call Zethunia. A voice answered, "UH! What you want?" It had to be Zefunia, only a Kap'p i would answer any communication in such a way.

"This is Maradish and would like to come and see you, it seems we both have lost our love ones."

"He only lost to universe not to Zefunia, but come if you must."

"Thank you. May I come, perhaps help with your festivities."

"Come to gate only. Need instruct for entry. Coordinate 87 02 56 72".

"Will do." The conversation was abruptly ended, Zefunia apparently had nothing else to say so simply disconnected.

Maradish packed her air car, set all the security devises and left the farm and farmhouse, unsure about what if anything would be accomplished by this visit. About half way, she stopped at a small lodge for the night. Again she attempted to eat but after only a few bites pushed it aside and retired to her room.

Early the next morning, after another restless night, she did not bother even to order a breakfast but went directly to her car and resumed trip. She arrived at the coordinates early in the afternoon. It appeared to be a common looking wood rail fence with a single gate but the instruments in her air car indicated there was an electronic barrier along the fence. The gate appeared to be of very simplistic design, perhaps to confuse any intruder, on a post was a single button. Maradish pushed the button and a voice seemingly from nowhere said, "UH What you want?"

"Maradish need instructions to see you."

"Under button, panel, enter code T 456 JPD 7, when enter, have twenty seconds through gate, all void after. Stay on path, close to ground, not drift off, follow to house."

"OK see you in little while", said Maradish but had the impression she was just talking to herself. As she pressed the last number of the code the gate disappeared, she hurriedly got back into her car and drove down the pathway remaining, as instructed, close to the ground. She turned her head around to look and the gate had reappeared.

The pathway was lined on both sides with a variety of flowers , bushes and trees, all nicely trimmed and well cared. She began to think about the talk of the immense wealth of Taygo, how he had made it moving merchandise between his home planet AND Traket. He had become one of the richest individuals in the Empire at the time. It was talk, no one could ever confirmed it as talk or could confirm it as a fact.

She traveled the path for two or three miles before she came up and on a small hill, the pathway ended as she reached the top the hill what she saw almost took her breath away. Below was a large open area with one large house still a distance away, almost in the middle of what appeared to be a huge pasture. To the right were numerous Ya' grum, (a bovine type animal covered with long shaggy red hair), and to the left several large herds of Boshmues, (similar to the American Buffalo but larger) and just beyond them were what appeared to be over a hundred Cutif'kil (similar the wild pigs). Scattered about there appeared to be fields of all kinds of cultivated plants and individuals working in many of them. She continued toward the house, it was quite apparent that Taygo was a very successful rancher and very rich indeed! Beyond all the animals were houses which she learned later were homes for all the servants and workers.

Closer to the house she observed surrounding the house was a very large, well manicured lawn with more than several workers busy cutting, trimming and planting different types of foliage. Not one seemed to give any attention to her as she stopped the car in front of the house. Before she was able to open the door of the car, three individuals were through the large double doors on the front of the house and were down the marble steps to assist her. One was around the car and opened the door, took hold of her hand to help her out of the car. The second quickly retrieved her luggage and the third, when Maradish was out the car, got in and drove it around the corner to a garage for servicing and storage until she would be ready to return to her place of residence.

Escorted by the first, they walked up the marble steps, they reached about half way up the steps when the door once more opened, it was Zefunia and she stepped out, but only a step or two. Along with her and one on either side were two exact duplicates of her only much smaller. Zefunia said with a loud voice, "You here! Come in, this is Bralafi," Pointing to the one left of her, "And this is Himopic." Pointing to the other one.

"Very glad to meet you," replied Maradish wondering how she could tell them apart, they looked exactly alike to her and all three looked exactly like Taygo.

The six of them entered the house, the one with her luggage without a word being said hurried up a set of stairs to the second floor, the one escorting her left and disappeared toward the back of the house. They were left in a large entry lobby with several doors and a large staircase leading upstairs. The lobby was beautifully decorated with what appeared to be articles and furnishings from many different planets of the "Empire".

"Go," said Zefunia to her children and both disappeared toward a room to one side of the lobby. "We go to study," she continued sounding more like an order than a request. They went toward two large doors and as they approached, the doors opened. Maradish entered first and walked into a spacious room with shelves filling two walls, elegantly furnished with what appeared costly items from all over the "Empire". As Zefunia entered the doors closed behind her and she reached to one of the shelves, removed some documents, opened a small panel and flipped a switch.

"Now!" Said Zefunia, "No one hear. Sound suppressor. What you want?" The roughness of her voice, typical of a Kap'pi but seemed more rough than usual caught Maradish off guard. "I know you not here to mourn for my Taygo. Very familiar with Kap'pi. So why you here?"

Maradish recovered quickly and said, "Stafic is alive and we need to know for sure Taygo is OK."

"We know Stafic OK. Both in hiding for present." Her voice more mellow now.

"The last time I saw Stafic we did not know for sure so he sent me to inquire."

"OK accept. Taygo instruct, I give envelope. You go D'Jaricta. Open after arrive. Will destruct thirty second after open also contact Caruthian."

Maradish knew not to ask about the envelope, just follow the instructions and see later why.

"Tell Stafic when see, most glad both good. Much power involved. We make festivity for Taygo. You stay." It did sound as if it was a request and not an order. Without another word Zefunia had flipped the switch back, replaced the documents and was walking out the door, Maradish had no recourse but to follow, the doors shutting behind her as she left the study.

The festivity for the death of Taygo was to be in three days and expected to last for a week. Guests would begin to arrive in two and including many of the rich and powerful of the Empire. Ambassadors from other planets, government officials , the heads of their various departments and even the close associate and confident of the Emperor himself. It was every apparent Taygo was respected and possibly feared by many influential individuals of the Empire. It was very possible the very one responsible for the "death" of Taygo was among the guests. Zefunia and Maradish agreed they were to observe for some action or talk of the possible culprit of the trouble. Only the one responsible would know there was any kind of trouble in the organization itself.

The festivities would be with much food and drink, music and dancing, it was to be a most happy time for everyone who knew him especially his direct family. The Kap'pi believed the departed were now in a better place and therefore rejoicing was in order.

When the last of the guests departed, Maradish waited another day and also left, returning to her farm which seemed so small and drab in comparison to where she had just been.

VII

Maradish was back at her farm and was unpacking when the radio crackled to life, she did not recognize the voice of the dispatcher. "Maradish. This is Prokliter. Sorry about your loss but we have an assignment for you. The mission will be for six weeks."

Maradish answered, "Not for sure I want another mission, very seriously thinking about retiring."

"Understand. Of course, that will be your choice Please consider and think about it we must have an answer in two weeks, your team leader will be Zennium and he has already said you would be more than alright."

"I'll try and let you know in time but for the next week or two, I am leaving for only peace and quiet. When I return I'll let you know if someone else is to take my place. While I decide, I would be most upset if anyone were to follow me to keep tabs or any other reason!"

"There is reason for that, you off duty time is your business," Was the reply. "Are you planning to go someplace?"

"Yes. For a week or ten days."

"Where are going so that we may contact of there is a problem."

"THAT IS EXACTLY what I don't want. I do not want to be disturbed until I return. DO I MAKE MYSELF CLEAR!" She disconnected without further comment.

Was it just a coincidence the call came at the precise time she arrived back from being with Zefunia or was someone watching her movements all the time? The latter was unnerving, she had NOT noticed anyone following her but she WOULD be more aware from this time until…. If it were so, they were able to avoid what all agents were trained to detect. If that were so, she would have to be extra careful of who she spoke with and what she did.

She finished the unpacking , decided to fix her something to eat and went to the kitchen. She entered the room and was startled to see Stafic, calmly stirring something on the stove.

"Been waiting for you," He said flatly. "Was getting pretty hungry, thought I might have to come and get you."

"Wha what are you doing here?"

"Aren't glad to see me?" He said dejectedly.

Suddenly she regained her composure and ran to him, nearly knocking him off his feet as she grabbed him in a furious bear hug.

"I take it you are glad," Grasping for breath. "But why are you trying to kill me again?"

She released him , "NO. NO, of course not. But how did you get through all the security?"

"Did you forget me that quick. I have been eluding security devises for ten years. It's my stock and trade. Besides you gave me all the codes."

"Of course, I should have remembered, just a memory lapse, I guess. That is what Zefunia meant when she said WHEN you see Stafic."

"Lets eat, I am starved."

"Me too, but not for food."

"Later sweet, right now let's eat while it is still hot."

They sat down to eat, she only sat looking at him, almost absent mindedly stirring at her food. "You don't like what I fixed?"

"Of course." She began to nibble at the food.

"While we're eating I'll explain why I am here. First, have heard all your calls including the one that just came in. You need to accept the assignment. Wait till you return from your vacation. I know you are to go to D'Jaricta for that vacation. Be careful while there you may be watched. Follow the instructions in the envelope, you'll be meeting with a Carputhion."

"I am almost positive I am being watched very closely, it is very unnerving because I have not been able to detect who or even how. I will be so glad when all this will be over."

" Taygo has sleeper contacts in the government keeps us informed, this assignment you have been selected for, has been in the works for a long time before you went to see Zefunia and it may be the final showdown, the make or break for the Organization, if you will. They also knew about your trip to see Zefunia and waited until you came back to tell you about it. At first, they did not know why but when you were there to celebrate the passing of Taygo, they believed it was the only reason for the trip. Taygo WAS your team leader!"

"Sweet," Maradish began reluctantly. "Was it not decided the behind all this HAD to be a very powerful individual?"

"Yes."

"I really hate to even think this but I just came from one very powerful person, knows the tactics, has inside information both in the Organization and the government."

"You can't honestly believe what you are saying, can you?" "I honestly don't want to but you did not observe all the powerful ones at the festivities. Not to mention if everyone believes him to be dead, what better cover?"

"I can see the logic but what would he have to gain?"

"That I don't know."

"It means, if you are right, there is nothing we can or plan to do. We will have to watch and see one way or another. Another thing, there WILL be another attempt on my life, HE DOES know I am still alive!"

"When will we be able to return to our lives again?"

"That I can't say, it will be back to the normal or the total disbanding of the Organization. What we agree on, is the one behind it all is either very powerful or has a lot of influence, whomever it is, he or she or they, it may have the backing of the Empire. What I don't understand. IF the Emperor wanted the Organization disbanded, all he would have to do is sign an order and withdraw all funding."

They completed the rest of the meal in silence, each thinking or wondering what was next. With the meal complete, Stafic reluctantly said, "Well it is time to disappear again, will attempt to keep in touch as often as possible."

"Do you have to leave right now?"

"I must say yes, the longer I stay around you the harder it is to leave and that could be disastrous for both of us."

"Do you HAVE to leave RIGHT now?" said Maradish in almost a whisper.

"Well. Maybe I can stay a little longer," replied Stafic taking the hint. Both walked arm in arm out the kitchen and toward the bedroom.

Later that day, Stafic left but at least this time Maradish was not in tears as before, sad to be sure but knew it was best for both of them and knew also her Stafic was alive and would to everything he could to remain alive and they, when this was over, would be together again.

Maradish waited two days and called. "Decided to accept the mission but only after I take about a week to ten days vacation. I'll be without a radio and I don't want to be in contact with anyone."

"Where will you go?"

Then she said as roughly as possible, " I'LL TELL YOU AGAIN THAT is exactly what I don't want, I don't want ANYONE to know where or what I do for this week. I GOT to get my head on straight before I go on ANY mission and I want absolutely no interference or anyone to assist or know where or even exactly when I return, IS THAT CLEAR? If there is the slightest indication of anyone around me to observe, the entire mission as far as I am concerned can be terminated and I WILL retire immediately! Is THAT clear!"

"Absolutely. I will inform my superiors but I do not think they will like being completely out of touch with you."

"I really don't care if they like it or not, those are my terms. Take it or leave it!" She continued with a very irritated voice. "Just remember I HAVE ability to detect if anyone is following me, through all the many years it has kept me alive and I WILL take a very dim view of any type of interference. DO I MAKE MYSELF PERFECTLY CLEAR?"

"Yes, very clear. Give me two days to confirm."

"Confirm or not, I DON"T CARE! It is either my way or no way, I can and will retire right now, this conversation is over, OUT!!" As soon as she finished she disconnected the link.

The very fact of the fierce temperament of her kind was all that should have been needed but she decided to be a little more persuasiveness to make sure no one try to follow her "on her vacation". She also realized they most likely would attempt to follow her in order to keep her from disappearing completely.

Later that day, the radio crackled to life. "Maradish," it was one she had talking with. "It is agreed to accept your proposal. Call when you return for details of the mission."

Maradish smiled but answered with a rough disapproving voice, "IT WAS NOT a proposal, I will talk to you when I return."

She surmised it must be one maybe two individuals involved in this, there was not enough time, in her opinion, to get the approval from several even by radio communications. Anything to do with the government always traveled at a snails pace, there had to be discussions and counter proposals, etc. Nothing was ever done with any expediency and without conditions. The decision should have not arrived until just before the time mentioned was about to expire.

That taken care of, she again packed again for a trip which would different from the one from which she had just returned. This time she packed her weapons, she was allowed by treaty and she wanted anyone who may try to follow to know she was ready to, if necessary, eliminate any interference. It was not that she did not trust those involved, it was just she did not trust them, period. This had become a conflict of survival, on the one hand, power and backing, apparently, of the government and on the other hand skill and know how, to stay alive in a hostile environment. Packed and ready to go, she set the coordinates of D'Jaricta, started the engine of her air car, set it on automatic and the car lifted into the air, once clear of her security devises she reset them and she was on her way.

VIII

Airborne, with controls set on automatic, speed set at below normal cruise, she had little to do for the next six and half hours but watch the peaceful scenery go by, but her training and experience has taught her to not take anything for granted or for what it appeared. Alert, although an agreement had been made did not mean that the agreement would be kept. She was dealing with someone who did not care and would not hesitate to use any means possible to achieve its' own purpose. Whatever that purpose might be and had the "power" to accomplish it.

She had been in route for about an hour, she turned several unnecessary turns of different directions and observed on her onboard system a single craft following just out of visual sight the same turns. To ascertain if the one was indeed following her she made several more changes in direction, her system still indicated it also made the same turns. She fastened her safety harness more securely and pressed "invasive maneuver" on the panel. Immediately the air car went into a steep climb, rolled over and was headed in a opposite direction with increased speed but only for a few seconds before turning different direction and turning again, increasing speed changed direction again. She was headed directly at the suspected tracker, the distance between the two rapidly deteriorated before suddenly it turned abruptly barely avoiding a head on collision. With the increased speed, the car made one more maneuver and was behind the one following. The one following dove down, turned completely around and headed back the way in came. With a second press of the button the air car resumed its' leisurely course on to the destination. Maradish smiled and thought, if it was someone tailing her, maybe they got the picture, if it was not, the individual in the car must have thought she was some kind of crazy and best get away as quick and far as possible. In either case IT was no longer following her.

She was still not fully convinced she was not being followed even though the tracker system was not indicating anyone, made several turns of a different directions, reversing direction, increasing speed or slowing to almost a crawl before arriving at D'Jaricta from a direction opposite from a direct course from her farm to the town. What should have taken six and half hours, took slightly more than eight but she was confident no one had followed her. The sun was setting when she arrived.

D'Jaricta was a place for just relaxing, here and several other places were known generally by the governmental members of the Empire. It was apparent, although there was supposed to be no one following her, they could have already placed someone here. There was only a few places for sightseeing, the city promoted its' parks and nature trails as the main attractions for relaxation.

Maradish arrived and immediately checked into the only hotel in the city. With the claim of a long and tiring trip, she went directly to her assigned room. Once inside, she used a scanner to scan from any listening or visual devices. With the years of experience, she had learned never to assume anything is as it looks, it had kept her alive in some of the most difficult situations.

Satisfied there were no listening or visual devises, she held the envelope given her by Zefunia over the wash basin, opened and read the contents. It had only the words, "old city hall, room ten, eleven o'clock". Thirty seconds later the letter began to smolder and burn, leaving only a few ashes, these she washed down the drain. She thought to herself, "Never give all the information at once or right away." There was nothing to do but relax until the next day, so she went to the restaurant in the hotel for a bite to eat. As she ate, she causally look around the room, any one or more could be watching her and every move she made. There was no sense in worrying about who it might be, she thought she needed to do something as Stafic had said to keep them off guard and guessing, something she normally would NOT do, but what? Right now she wanted to enjoy her meal. No one would bother her, the quick temper of her kind was well known AND she WAS wearing a weapon. Her meal complete, she decided to do what was not expected, she would take a walk outside. If there were any suppose to keep watch on her maybe, just maybe, they would follow. Even if they were to keep their distance, she may get a glimpse and that is all she would need. As she left the restaurant and walked out the door into the cool night air, she could hear the movement and rustle from a table. Acting as if she didn't hear or care, she stepped out onto the walkway and began a slow walk toward nowhere in particular, just a walk.

She knew that they had to know the night was when she was at her best . If they had any inclination about keeping tabs on her, they would have to somehow follow. If followed and she caught even a glimpse she would then have an idea of the type or species assigned to shadow her and she could make the necessary adjustments to her contact with the Caruthion.

As she slowly walked along, there were two individuals exits the restaurant, unable to clearly determine the species or even the gender, she stopped, stretched and took several deep breaths, gazed up at the stars and slowly continued her walk. She noticed they appeared to discuss something and one walked to opposite direction away from her. The other began to walk her direction, she turned around and walked back toward the restaurant and hotel. They passed each other, Maradish took notice, it was a male, a Trakite, dressed in the normal attire of the peoples of this planet, but something was different. Not willing to divulge she even noticed, she casually walked on and entered the hotel. She continued to her room but the thing, whatever it was, bothered her. "What was it?"

She proceeded to make ready and go to bed, but not before placing a small motion detector next to the door. If the door moved the slightest, an alarm would immediately sound. She had another restless night, it seems all her nights were restless for one reason or another. A couple hours of turning and tossing, she suddenly sat straight up in her bed. "That is what it was!" She exclaimed to herself. "That male was carrying a weapon!"

Trakite law prohibited any civilian to carry any kind of weapon beyond a simple pocket knife. Only the military was allowed a weapon but even then was limited to military formations. She was allowed only because of the treaty which supersedes the law for "normal" individuals of Traket. Was the military involved? It could they are here to only follow orders and may not even know why they were told to follow her.

Morning finally came, after breakfast she again left for a causal walk. This time it was to see where the various places were in the city but also to time the walk to the city hall. It would be imperative she arrive and the designated spot at the designated time. If off by any appreciable time, the contact would have disappeared, a different rendezvous would be necessary. In this line of work, secrecy and timing was very critical. If she was being followed, they were very good, it was the possibility, the two were exchanging positions to make her think there was no one following. She did not obtain a good look at the other one but what she did see, there was only a brief glimpse once in a while. She began to wonder, if perhaps, whoever is behind all this may think she may be here for some other reason than the rest she had said she needed, if so, it would require extra caution. Her "shadows" were good but will, if she desired, at the right time, be left wondering where she had gone.

The clock in the tower of the new city hall indicated the time. The old city hall was one of the few sightseeing places in the city. The city proudly claimed it was built before the civil wars and one of the only buildings left standing from that time period. If it were true, which many thought very doubtful, it would have to be more than several centuries old.

Maradish causally strolled along the various shops, looking in the windows at the various items for sale to the tourists, slowly moving toward the old court house. The courthouse clock indicated it was ten minutes before eleven when Maradish began to walk up the marble steps of the old court house. She approached the two large wooden doors, stopping to admire the intricate carvings on the outside. When she began to open the door, she discovered it to swing very easily and quietly. In her mind she thought this could be bad, someone would be able to enter and she would not hear it open . But again, it WAS the only door available to enter and exit, so why would the one following her want to do that and risk being discovered. Why not just wait for her to exit.   She entered a long hallway, the walls were paneled with what appeared to be rich and expensive wood, adorned with pictures, she assumed were past governors, political figures or such; the floor was highly polished stone of some kind. She glanced around but saw no security cameras or detection devises, it did not mean they were not there, maybe just so well hidden they were unobserved by her.

She had about three minutes to find room ten. The rooms appeared to be numbered, odd numbers on the right and even numbers on the left. Without the knowledge of how many rooms were on this floor and the possibility of the room on the second floor, she moved a little faster down the hallway. Room ten was on this floor however it was the last one in the hallway. She entered the room as she heard the clock on the tower begin to chime, eleven o'clock.

The room was larger than she expected. Across the entire width was a bar with papers and folders neatly stacked at various places, across the back of the room were shelves from the floor to almost the ceiling filled with folders and various sizes of books, several desks and chairs scattered around the area between the bar and the shelves. Across from the bar was a line of chairs, all neatly lined and properly spaced along the wall. As she looked around there was no one present, it did seem it was kept clean and well dusted. She began to wonder is it all had been some kind of joke when she saw on one of the chairs an envelope. She carefully picked it up, there appeared no one watching. Upon opening the envelope there was another note inside. "This will self destruct in ten seconds. Department store. Cosmetics, ointments, three o'clock." Suddenly the paper and envelope smoldered and began to burn. In a matter of seconds everything was completely gone, without even an ash to be disposed.

She left the court house the way she entered, not in any hurry and causally, she walked back to the restaurant at the hotel. She ate her dinner meal quietly and slowly before leaving the restaurant and walking toward the park area, acting more like a tourist than what she actually was, an agent for the organization. Her action was more for the one or ones watching, if indeed they were any watching. If they were, they were very good at their job but by the same token they could be any one of the many "tourist" in the city, to be discovered would require a huge mistake on their part. As she approached the park, she stopped, looked and saw the department store. She hesitated as if thinking about something, then changed directions toward the department store, the tallest building in the city.

Still vigilant for any indication of anyone following her, her experience and training always stressed the ever present of danger or exposure. She had stopped, as any good tourist would, to look at the height of the building. It seemed so much taller than anything around, it stood out like a fox among a flock of hens.

She nearly jumped when a voice suddenly said, "Who would ever imagine such a tall building in such a small town." She turned to see the individual speaking, it was an Okmerish, presumably a tourist. She turned back, like a typical tourist, to look at the building,

"Yes, who would think," she replied in an absent minded fashion. "Must be a very popular place."

"Word is," said the Okmerish. "You can purchase ANYTHING in there." He emphasized anything.

"Really? Wonder if they have the special cream for MY skin, I must have sent in from my home planet."

"No harm in trying."

She started toward the building, turned to thank him for the information, also curious why he should place so much emphasis on the word anything, he was not there, he had disappeared, it was as if he was never there. To have anyone be so close to her and THEN suddenly disappear was unnerving. Maradish was now more on edge, who was that person and why did he suddenly appear and just as suddenly disappear?

She entered the department store and was in a large room filled with all kinds of damaged, returned and discontinued items. (Here on earth would be called a bargain basement). The items filled tables and shelves, she turned to leave thinking she had maybe entered the wrong door, when a Trakite, a male ask, "May I direct you to your pleasure?"

"Yes, I am in need of an ointment for my skin."

"Very good," he replied in a monotone. "If you please enter the lift to your right. To the third floor, on you left is cosmetics, ointments and perfumes. Perhaps they will have what you seek."

She entered the lift and along with several others was lifted upward. When it arrived at the third floor, Maradish and two others got off, the rest continued upward after the door closed. Turning her left, she walked into a room which appeared to filled with females for all over the Empire. She began looking for a Caruthion, at least that was the individual she was told would be her contact. She began to wonder just how, IF her contact was here, with the crowd, how she would know or was this another "message" contact. As she looked around and observed the crowd which appeared to be all if not mostly female. On the assumption her contact must be a female, she began to walk to see if there was a Caruthion anywhere.

The Caruthion are from a female dominated planet in the system called Xmmertin, pale green in color, the females are larger in body mass and taller than the male and it is rumored are able to control any male with their mind. This is not accepted by the general public and believe their size was the way of advantage and control, this thought was not discouraged by the female Caruthions.

There were females of all sizes and various skin colors or at least they all appeared to be females, there was even a female from her planet, Tyrunic. Although Maradish was not carrying a weapon, the other one was, therefore, it was best to remain well clear of her. Maradish moved to a counter and began to examine the merchandise . A short and plump, tan colored female, a Quewitin, only about half the height of Maradish, approached her and said, "May I be of assistance?"

"Yes. I need a jar of Pezifnic ointment."

"Very good. You will find ointments on aisle twelve, I am sure they will be happy to assist you."

"THANK YOU!" She responded roughly in keeping with her species. She found her way to aisle twelve and as she approached, she observed another Tyrunic, she also was carrying a weapon, this one was examining facial articles which are never worn by her kind. Curious, but not curious enough to ask why and stir the ire of a Tyrunic, especially one with a weapon. Aisle twelve, there were three females behind the counter and two on her side trying various ointments on their skin. She walked to the counter and a pale, thin female ask, "May I help you?"

"Do you have any Pezifnic ointment?"

"It is very difficult to obtain and rare, we don't keep it on the shelf, it is so perishable, at present we are out of stock."

"Thank You!" Replied Maradish gruffly. "I was told I could find ANYTHING, I GUESS that person was WRONG!"

A Caruthion also behind the counter spoke, "Dewthica, if you please finish with this customer. We would not want anyone to not be happy when they leave, perhaps I know something that may please her. I am very familiar about the type of ointment Tyrunic require. Let me see if I can help her." Dewthica went to assist the other customer. The name tag the Caruthion was wearing indicated her name to be Chabmoda and she said, "Perhaps I will be able to help you."

"Not actually, I needed the rest so I came here on vacation and did not realize I was low on my ointment. If the Pezifnic is not available I will HAVE to terminate my vacation."

"Vacation? (Vacation from a Tyrunic was the code word). We would NOT want you to do that. If rest is what you seek, our parks are a wonderful place to rest especially around the fountain, it is most soothing," said Chabmoda as she was taking several jars off a shelf. "But for your immediate needs perhaps we can help you. Our chemists have developed several ointments which duplicate the Pezifnic and have over twice the shelf life and one third the price. We even have many but here are eight different aromas from which to choose. Note the size of the jar is twice the size of the Pezifnic.

Maradish began to causally look at bottles of ointments.

Chabmoda gave a very slight nod of the head and Maradish picked one and sniffed the contents. Chabmoda continued, "Notice if you will the beautiful aroma, it will excite the most difficult male."

"I don't need any aroma to excite a male but it does smell very delectable not anything like Pezifnic. Outside the attraction for a male, what I need to know will it help my skin?"

"Most positively, the basic compound is the same if not better than the Pezifnic."

"What does a jar cost?"

"It cost only thirty credits, try it and if it does not do what you desire, bring it back and we will return your cost plus ten percent for your trouble."

"Can't go very wrong with that." Maradish paid the thirty credits and left with the knowledge of where their next meeting would take place, in the park, next to a fountain at eight o'clock, she would be with another individual. Who would be with her? Her next obstacle was to have the meeting without anyone knowing. It would take her training and experience to outmaneuver her shadow, not for sure if there was only one or if there was more than one. Her shadow or shadows were very good however they had the cover of numerous individuals around. They would not have THAT cover tonight. Maradish left the department building and decided to have a walk around in the park, she needed to know the general location of her destination and access to it without being seen. She left the park and walked causally along the avenue, looking at the various shops. She noticed one individual appear to stop when she stopped and move as she moved, she made it a point to act as if she did not observe the movements of the other. She was hoping to be able to get the individual close enough to see the species or at least the gender. She reached the hotel without successfully identifying the shadow so because it was almost suppertime went directly to the restaurant. Because of the number of those entering and leaving the restaurant, she discontinued her attempt to identify her shadow. After eating she went directly to her room, scanned for any hidden visual or audio devises, then settled down for a rest and wait for the night.

When time to leave, she would leave through the front door. She would exit as a tourist and not dressed for stealth. She would be wearing her black slacks and black sneakers but a colorful top. It would be the top she had designed for herself years ago for a similar operation and several afterward,   colorful on one side but quick reversible to black on the other side. The design only required a few seconds to accomplish the change, obtaining that few seconds was always the challenge.   The sun was due to set at six o'clock, without a moon it would be dark by seven. With this in mind, Maradish determined to leave before seven and walk causally as possible, enjoying the cool night air. But for now, it was it was her rest time.

The clock indicated six thirty, Maradish calmly dressed for the game of cat and mouse about to begin. From all outward indications, as she walked out of her room, she was just going for another nighttime stroll after all she WAS on vacation.

She walked slowly along the well lit streets of the city not stopping to look at anything but did stop periodically and take a deep breath as if enjoying the cool fresh air. When she stopped, she saw another someone following at a distance, also walking at about the same pace as she. She finally caught a glimpse of her shadow.

She walked at first away from the park but gradually turned in its' direction until finally entering into the park. Stepping along a path, she came to a bend, she walk slowly around the bend and was out of view of her shadow. In less than five seconds, she was out of her top, had it turned and back on, a second later she disappeared into the trees. She could have waited there for her shadow to appear but instead she began to make her way to the rendezvous with Chabmoda.

Maradish approached the fountain, on a bench was Chabmoda and she had a baby carriage with her, was that the other person? With use of her skill in stealth, she approached the Caruthian and was close enough to reach and touch her, checked to see if there were any others within audio range before quietly said, "Chabmoda."

The sound of a voice so close caused Chabmoda to almost jump up. "I was told of your skill," she whispered as she settled back. "But had no idea you were THAT good. Your assignment will be to Facitisha and I will meet you there you'll be staying at the Grand Royal hotel."

"How will I know when you arrive?"

 "Don't worry, YOU WILL know."

Puzzled as how it might be accomplished and thinking a clue may be in the child somehow, she asked, "You have a child?" To have a child was not in keeping with single agents, with always the possibly go on a mission and never come back.

"No", Chabmoda giggled. "It isn't real, just part of my cover, we will be working close together and a real child would be in the way. One more thing, you are being followed."

"I know. Better return to being a tourist before my shadow gets worried. See you at Facitisha." Maradish disappeared into the darkness of the trees, emerged on a path on the side away from the fountain and was slowly walking back toward the hotel when her shadow emerged, quickly looked around before seeing her.

Maradish remained for another three days before she checked out of the hotel and had a easy and relaxing trip back to the farm.

IX

Maradish arrived at her farm and began to unpack her belongings when she smelled a particular odor. Unsure what exactly it might be, she picked up her hand weapon and began to trace where the odor was coming from and especially what or who was causing it. She traced to the kitchen, she tensed her body and suddenly burst through the door ready for anything.

"Is that anyway to welcome a friend?" Said Stafic, calmly, standing near the stove stirring in a pot. "After all, I have been waiting a long time and cooking one of your favorites too."

She temporarily stunned to see him but recovered quickly with a scream, dropped her weapon, rushed to him, nearly knocking him off his feet. With a hug almost taking his breath away and kisses, he could barely ask, "Are you trying to kill me, AGAIN?"

"Of course not, I am so glad to see you. The last few days have been so lonely for me. How did you know when I would return?"

"It has not been any picnic for me either. You have been under our watch. Remember we knew where you were going almost before you did."

After settling down, "Here sit down and eat, we have a lot of things to cover before I must go again."

"Later, I am more interested in something else, I am NOT taking any excuses or delays. Eating can wait!"

"If it will make you happy," he said with a big smile as he took her hand and they left the kitchen.

"You bet it will!" It was almost two hours later when they returned to the kitchen. As they walked through the door he was saying, "You know the food I prepared is probably cold and need to be reheated."

"That is alright, I can wait, "she replied smiling.

"I'll reheat the food, you need to call in and let them know you are back. They already know it but they don't want you to think they do. You know of course they had someone to follow you all the while you were gone?"

"Yes, I knew, had to shake it off while I met with Chabmoda. After that I didn't care if they followed or not."

" As far as we can determine they did NOT know about the meeting. Now go a let them know you are back and are ready for the assignment, while I heat our meal."

Maradish called the organization, "I am back and feel much better. I am ready for an assignment when you have one."

"Glad you are back. Hope you had a most relaxing time."

"Yes it was very relaxing! There was nothing to think about and nothing it particular to do. I had very serious thoughts of retiring and doing that for the rest of my life but then again I would tire of nothing to do in a very short time. SO, when the next assignment ?"

"The next one has been in the works for several months. Briefing is scheduled for next week. Departure is for a week after."

"Almost sounds as if you were positive I would accept an assignment."

"Not positive but very hopeful, it will be much easier with your expertise and abilities then to rely on another of less experience."

"Thanks for the vote of confidence, let me know the time and place of the briefing. Signing off."

The meal was reheated and served but both only sat looking at it, wondering what would be the results of all the intrigue and deception.

Stafic was the first to speak, "We really need to discuss what is now in the works and what it is we think will be the results."

"I really don't want to speculate but I also know we all need to know what is happening, our very livelihood and perhaps even out lives depend on everyone being informed."

"We know from our contacts, the assignment is for Facitisha, with Taygo and myself out of the way, believe Zennim and his top agents are next and targeted for elimination somehow but before they can do it will hopefully expose who and why we are being disbanded it this particular way. For reason or reasons yet to be discovered, you are the in the center of it all. As we are speaking, every agent and their families are being transported to Faitisha and from there will only depend on what happens there. Most want to just melt into the populations they came from, for the time being it is deemed not advisable. We believe they would be hunted down and exterminated, one by one. The government has too many undercover agents scattered in all the populations. There HAS to be a way they can all return without fear of exposure and death, myself, that is another question, unanswerable at present. I may have to for the safety of the others be sacrificed."

"NO! NO! I won't let them do that. We will work out something!" She cried with tears in her eyes.

"That my sweet is the way things are at present, the next move is you on assignment."

"I won't go if it means I lose you!"

"It is what you must do. If possible maybe something can be worked out but you must help us get to the bottom of this."

"Places a lot on what I do and how I do it," Tears still in her eyes.

"Don't try to do anything you would not ordinarily do, just be yourself. To do something out of character may cause suspicion or even a change of intentions. As of now we are being informed, if they change we will have to act in the blind. It is time for me to again disappear. Look for me, I may be where you lease suspect. Don't forget I LOVE YOU." With the last comment, Stafic once more disappeared into the darkness of the night.

At the briefing a week later, the team learned the particulars of the mission and a new development in defensive strategy of the target, the implementation of a different type of detection device. It was a different type of particle beam, its exact composition unclear. Because of this the scientist could not develop a means of "seeing" the beams therefore were unsure of the extent or pattern the beams or how to defeat it. There may be a way of scrambling the program if the location of the computer was known. This development was unnerving to Maradish, it meant she had a complete unknown. She always had an unknown to deal with but she did not like not knowing or at least have a suspect of knowing. The team received the orders, the team would arrive at Faitisha on three different transports and stay at two different hotels. All weapons and associated equipment was either already there or would arrive within the forty eight hours before the mission was to begin. Each of them was given the necessary documentation for their cover and tickets for the transports. All that was left to do is board their designated flights for the two hundred forty eight hour flight. The cover for Maradish was one she used several times before and one she was well acquainted, seller of exotic foods mostly for kings, in this case for the "Kings Banquet". Her job, after selling them, was to insure ALL the foods arrive on time and properly stored and ready to be properly prepared. This particular "Kings Banquet" was for the marriage of the king and his "new" bride which happened to be his sixth of his harem.

X

Maradish arrived at the terminal dressed in a formal suit and carrying a briefcase filled with documents from many planets, with instructions for preparing and serving plus full color and descriptions of how these most rare and exotic foods from all over the Empire were supposed to look when properly prepared. Although allowed to do so, she carried no weapon on her person or in the briefcase. Her destination was NOT part of the Empire, therefore not subject to any treaty, without a weapon it would enable her to pass through customs more easily. The purpose "officially" was a trade mission and attendance at the kings wedding ceremony and banquet and also to show off the many advantages of being a member of the Empire. Up to this time the king had not shown any interest in becoming a member but still enjoyed the trade, attention and income from the Empire. The king ignored the numerous warnings of impeding assassination believing it was just one of the many he received since becoming king and it was something every king must take with a grain of salt to be king.

Maradish waited in the waiting area for loading to begin, each passenger was assigned a specific seat on the transport and would begin transportation by way of an intra-atmospheric craft to the waiting transport in stationary orbit above the terminal. She attempted and without being very noticeable, scanned the various passengers about to board. She noticed another Tyunic, appeared to be a male plus various others from over the Empire.   The Tyunic appeared to be talking with a short, gray individual with long black hair which covered its entire head even to the point of obscuring its face. She smiled to herself and wondered how it could see where it was or where it was going. The flight number was called and boarding began. As she began to walk to the craft, she noticed a Doldit. Immediately there rose within her the long suppressed hatred, from deep within her being a growl emerged. The growl surprised her, she thought she had overcome any display of emotions about ANY species.

Doldic is an all white individual, as much white as a Tyunic was black, a strict pacifist, able to even give up its' liberty or that of any other instead of indulge in any type violence. It was this attitude, is detested by almost every species, had cost the lives of many including the Tyunic, none hated the Doldic more than the Tyunic. It was from the past when a Doldit, violated the trust of a group of Tyunic, who were all killed, it was interpreted as to save its own skin. To violate a trust was something the Tyunic could never understand. Thus a hatred for all Doldit and constant mistrust of anything they MIGHT do, continued to build over the centuries. The Doldit are tolerated by all EXCEPT the Tyunic, they refuse to associate with them in any fashion or form.   Maradish did not like the feeling, she thought she had eliminated it years ago. It could hinder her actions and anything that may slow or cause a hesitation in action could and often was the reason for becoming injured or killed.

She entered the cabin of the ship, watching the Doldit to make sure it would be as far a distance from her as possible. She noticed the other Tyunic was also watching close the Doldit. All seated and strapped in, take off and rendezvous with the transport was uneventful.

Because of limited space for passengers on the transport, two individuals were assigned to a room, each had to have their own seat for the initial jump and deceleration back to inter solar travel. Everyone had to be secure during these two periods, the rest of the flight were free to move about as needed.

As each entered the transport a seat number was given them, she took her number a move slowly along the very narrow aisle. There were two rows of seats and set in pairs. Her number indicated next to the wall with a seat next to her on the aisle. She took her place, fastened the restraints and settled for the jump. She watched as the cabin quickly began to fill with what appeared to be about twenty passengers. She closed her eyes to relax for the short period of time before the jump. She felt someone sit in the seat next to her, opened her eyes to greet the individual and saw the Doldit.

She instantly flew into a rage and shouted, "GET THIS CREATURE AWAY FROM ME!" She instinctively reached for her weapon. No weapon was available, "IF I HAD my weapon I would kill this THING!" Two stewards moved as quick as possible to the disturbance.

"If you don't get it out my sight I will kill it with my bare hands!" She continued to shout. Her movement toward the Doldit, he, it was a male, move out of the way, Maradish was restricted by the restraints.   A steward reached the two and immediately began to apologize, "We are so sorry, we will move him away immediately , there must have been a foul up in scheduling."

"YOU BET THERE WAS!" Maradish continued to shout, "AND I don't care what you do with IT just get him away from me!"

A Bafkifion, a female, close to the front of the cabin ask, "Ish be alrike I take place?" The Bafkifion were one of the most friendly of the all the species but had difficulty saying many of the simplest words.

"Anything would be better than that THING!" Stated Maradish still fuming.

The Bafkifion and the Doldit exchanged positions and the stewards still apologizing made the proper entries into the computer to indicate the change.

Maradish during the disturbance noticed the Doldit had a weapon, what was a Doldit doing with a weapon?, she thought but said nothing.

"MY name ish Rafiron."

"Maradish"

"Pret nam."

"Thank you," replied Maradish calming down, the Bafkifon seemed to have that affect on many individuals.

The Bafkifion seemed to have the ability to create a calming affect, at will, on even the most difficult situations. They were slender with a tan complexion and nothing else outstanding in appearance. The one strange particularity was every five years their gender would change, males became female and visa versa. This reason was once mated together, it was for life.

Although limited in its sphere of influence, during the meetings of the government assembly, several were stationed at various areas of the most argumentative and disruptive members to calm tempers when words became to the point of getting out of hand. With an enhanced ability, as an agent it had the ability to place the adversary at ease and then with deadly force eliminate it. It made the Bafkifion agent both efficient and lethal.

It was not known how they acquired this ability but perhaps it had something to do with their diet. It was known that the young of them did not have this ability. It was only attained as the individual grew older and into adulthood.

The overhead speakers suddenly came to life with, "Secure all belongings. Make sure all restraints are as firmly in place as possible. Jump begins in sixty seconds." There was a sudden rush of noise as all loose items were secured and any who did not secure themselves before moved quickly to do so. As the craft went from cruise speed to jump speed anything or anybody not secured would be hurled toward the back of the cabin and hitting the back wall with the force of a thousand pound weight dropped from a hundred feet. The jump would last only five seconds and then the sense of moving would be non-existent. The jump occurred without incident and the occupants could now unbuckle their restraints.

As everyone began to move around, a steward approached Maradish and said softly and fearing the worse. "I am sorry but it seems the Doldit was also assigned to the same sleep quarters as you." "WHAT!" shouted Maradish, her temper once more on the rise. "What kind of operation do you run?" The steward continued sheepishly "Please, please we have made a change with your approval."

"It better be a good one."

"OH, yes that is if you will approve, if not we will do whatever possible to make you happy."

"WELL, WHAT IS IT?" Still irritated.

"It is the other Tyunic, would like to share sleep quarters with you."

"I BET HE WOULD. Tell him the quarters ONLY and NOTHING else. If he agrees, fine, if not stay where he is and find someone else like Rafiron here, matter of a fact, I think I would prefer Rafiron to anyone else."

"I mos sory, Mardis, I not able be wit you. I travil wit mate, we ned stay togeter."

"I can fully understand," said Maradish her voice once more very calm. "If I were traveling with my mate it would require an army to separate us." Shifting her attention to the steward, "See what you can do."

"Thank you, I will return shortly with his answer."

It was after the exercise period and the meal, when Maradish decided to retire to her assigned room. As she entered, she was startled to find the other Tyunic already there. Recovering quickly and still in the doorway, She glared at the male laying on one of the beds as if he already owned it. "DO YOU FULLY UNDERSTAND THE RESTRICTIONS," she growled

He barely moved but turned his head toward her and said in a low gruff voice, "You don't have to let everyone on the ship hear. There was no one else who would accept living with YOU for the next hour much less the next two hundred or more hours. So whether you like it or even don't want to accept it YOU are stuck with me."

"I guess I have little choice, I will tell you, IF you even attempt to do ANYTHING beyond staying on your side to this room, I am quite capable of inflicting severe injury."

"I am quite aware of the capability but you also keep in mind I have the same ability."

Maradish entered the rest of the way into the room and shut the door and sat on the edge of her bed, keeping a wary eye on the male, relaxing on the bed on the opposite side of the small room. He appeared to be fully relaxed and quite oblivious to her presence. She tried to relax but was unable because of the thought of him so very close to her.

"You know if you don't relax, you will be nothing but a bundle of nerves and possibly cause a major health problem."

"THAT is of no concern of yours", she retorted.

"OH, but that is where you are wrong! Mara, I could not stand to make you sick. I nursed you back to health once and would do it again but if it was me that made you sick….." As he spoke, he sat up on the edge of the bed.

"WHAT!" She interrupted and growled. "Where do you or more to the point why did you call me Mara?"

The Tyunic opened his jacket exposing a blue skin. It was Stafic. She sat stunned, her mouth dropped open. IT WAS Stafic! Her sense would not allow her to accept that her love was sitting on a bed opposite her.

She was almost in a state of shock until he said, "Well are you not glad to see me?"

Suddenly recovered, she screamed, "YES!"with one leap was across the room and on top him, knocking him backward."Yes!   Yes!" she repeated over and over nearly smothering him with kisses. Then just as sudden as she had leaped to him she stood up hands on her hips and growled, "What is the meaning you causing all that stress? Why are you acting like a Tyunic? How did you get to look like one?"

"Whoa! Whoa! And quiet down. These rooms are not completely sound proof. Let me answer one at a time."

"OK. Explain yourself!"

"First, Taygo and I had to somehow get to the planet. The only way was to disguise ourselves, remember we are both dead. Taygo decided to be a member of the music ensemble, in his case a Poffittican, myself a Tyunic, had it arranged for the Doldit to sit next to you so I would have the opportunity to travel WITH you to Faitisha. It took some experimenting to cover my skin but finally found the right oil and then the other additions to look like one of your kind, which I might say is quite uncomfortable. It was little trouble to act but to sound like a Tyunic is hard on my throat. That is it in a nutshell."

"WEELL, I guess I can forgive you THIS time but if you ever do it again...."

"I get the picture, hopefully I will never have the need. Also, the Doldit has been assigned to keep you under surveillance."

"By who?"

"That we have NOT been able to determine but firmly believe it is whoever is behind all this and may find out once you arrive on Faitisha."

"Now that is cleared, why don't we enjoy our time together?"

"I most heartily approve BUT outside this room it will necessary to be at each others throat."

"Only IF!"

"What are you waiting for a printed invitation."

"I'LL print you an invitation", she cooed as she climbed back into the bed with him.

For the next two hundred forty hours or so the charade continued, each being the professional they had been trained to be for the majority of the time, but alone was a most happy for the both of them. It was during one of their times alone, there was the following conversation.

"So you are a jewel expert" said Maradish with a smile.

"Would like to think so but I am only suppose to verify the arrival of the jewels and if any are missing to send for them, priority one, we still have two weeks before the wedding."

"How about I test your aptitude on jewels?" she replied with a big grin.

"Might be a way to pass the time."

"Alright, what is a blue crystal with glowing red bits inside?'

"Hmmm. That would be a roshmune."

"Good, that was an easy one , how about a clear crystal with scattered black stripes throughout?"

"That is a very rare one, but is called a defmora."

"What does a Ziizon look like?'

"Pale yellow, but it must be absolutely flawless."

"Very good. One more, what are the characteristics of a ekotuva?"

"It is bluish green in color with white uniformed bands evenly spaced around it."

"You have done your homework well, I think it about time for you to do so HOME work."

As the time approached for the arrival at Faitisha, Stafic thought it best to begin a briefing to inform Maradish of what was believed would take place once they were on the planet. It was not what he even wanted to think about because there was the possibility of him losing his beloved, something he never considered when they were both on Traket. It had turned into a life or death struggle between two forces, one of an unknown, only a possible origin.

"Mara, we will be arriving at Faitisha in less than twenty hours. I need to brief you on what we know, what to expect and what the outcome could be. It will be a difficult talk for me so please bear with me."

"OK, I have been expecting it and really need to know as much as possible before it begins."

"The first thing that needs to happen is I need to leave BEFORE you. I will try to be one of the first off, need you to delay as long as possible, be last if at all possible. There will be a disturbance at customs to delay you even more, the Doldit will most likely be waiting for you in the terminal somewhere. Don't be to concerned about him, he is supposed to follow but not harm you in any way."

"That is reassuring being I saw him carrying a weapon."

"REALLY! That was something we did not know. In the terminal look for a Vulakim, it will be a female, she will assist you in losing the Doldit. Only she knows just how she will do that. Just for your information, there are about fifty agents AND their families on Faitisha at present, she is one of them and is very capable at her work."

The Vulakim skin appears to be covered with wrinkles and the color of light tan and an average height of five to six feet, the female "normally" smaller than the male, they have a photographic memory and are able to provide even the smallest details of what they see.

"You were scheduled to be at the Grand Royal Hotel, you will not be staying there very long, you have been provided other accommodations, you know where when you get there. Only two of us know the location and that is because they know you are coming, when I say they I mean the ones you are suppose to eliminate. We believe there is some kind of trap set to capture you alive, which is the reason for the change of location, we have no idea when, how or more important where the trap will be."

"You are not providing me with much to go on."

"We did find that the new detection devise they have, is not some kind of light beam but a simple grid system to track your movements as you, as, they believe, you approach the banquet hall through the forest area. It is our plan to circumvent the grid and smuggle you into the building through the front door."

"WHAT AM I some kind of piece of furniture?"

"Not furniture but a musical instrument."

"That is even worse, I can't even carry a tune!"

"Try not worry, we will carry it for you."

"I don't like the idea but I also know there is little hope of changing YOUR mind."

Six hours, thirty minutes before the time of arrival, the speakers throughout the ship came to life announcing, "Secure ALL loose belongings, firmly secure yourselves to your assigned seat, deceleration will be in thirty minutes. Count down to deceleration begins immediately."

"Well here we go. Our countdown also begins, it now begins whether we like it or even want it or not," said Stafic very solemnly.

The countdown continued at ten minutes intervals , then one minute and finally seconds until with a huge explosive noise, everyone, even the securely fastened were strained against the bindings. Six hours later the craft docked at the orbiting satellite and the unloading of the passengers began onto a smaller landing craft for the twenty minutes flight to the terminal and customs.

Because he was a Tyrunic, it was easy for Stafic to nearly force his way on and then off the first landing craft and be one of the first to proceed through customs.

Maradish appeared to be in no hurry and simply sat waiting for the others to disembark. No one dared to ask her why she was waiting, fearing the ire of a Tyrunic. In a very relaxed sort of way, Maradish walked off the landing craft, the disturbance at customs was already in progress. As she walked into the terminal building, whatever the problem, it appeared to be resolved or at least mostly so. She was at the end of the line, she could see the customs officials were opening every piece of luggage and closely looking at nearly every article. It was very apparent they were looking for something, she was glad she did not have any kind of weapon on her person or stored within her luggage. She also saw the Doldit, no doubt waiting for her but walking slowly into the main part of the building. As she approached the official, she wondered how the Doldit went through customs WITH a weapon on his person? Her luggage was all opened and thoroughly checked, nothing of what they might have looking for, they closed the luggage and she was allowed to enter the large main area. Mirrored support pillars strategically placed throughout gave the huge room a sense of light coming from everywhere and be larger than it really was. She began her walk to the exit, on the lookout for her contact, the Vulakim, and keeping a watchful eye but also her distance from the Doldit. The Doldit was apparently or supposedly reading an article at a, what we would call a book store, but was called wunsaderpoct. It had a variety of written documents and visual recordings available for anyone interested.

Maradish saw her contact sitting on a bench calmly eating something. Maradish stopped to adjust her luggage, pretending the customs people, in their investigation, had made one of her cases hard to handle. The Vulakim saw her, already knew she was being followed. The task was to identify the pursuer. With her back directly toward the Doldit, she walked to one of the mirrored pillars, straightened her clothing and hair. Maradish walked to a snack bar, sit her case on the floor and ordered a thewpinin, a drink common throughout the Empire and being offered to those arriving for the festivities. The Vulaki watched as Maradish drank a few sips of the drink, went to pick up her case which opened and spilling the contents. Because of the known attitude of a Tyrunic no one offered to assist. One of first things she retrieved was a white article of clothing. The Vulakin got up and turned toward the bench and began adjust and pick up the articles on the bench. "If you are sure," was the indicated response. Maradish nodded her head slightly. It was hard to believe a Doltic would do anything but capitulate but the Vulakin shuffled a package to get a firm grip in acknowledgement.

Maradish hurriedly stuffed the case and got up and left. Without a word spoken the message was sent, received and confirmed. The Vulakin simply walked away and disappeared from sight.

When Maradsih reached the exit, for security reasons there was only one exit point, everyone was being visually checked and electronically scanned before leaving. Everyone had to pass through a revolving door with four guards on both sides, watching everyone coming in one side and leaving out the other.

The large door was divided into eight sections which enabled it to accommodate eight individuals at the same time, strictly controlled by the guards to keep a steady flow of individuals in and out. Maradish entered the line, she noticed the Vulakin carrying packages and was about fourth one behind her. She had somehow got between her and the Doltic. The Doltic was about three individuals behind her.

The door was in constant motion and the individual needed to step into the space provided and on to a moving platform which would carry the individual out of the terminal. Maradish stepped into the space, on the platform and in a few seconds was outside. As she stepped off the platform, the Vulakin was stepping on, miss stepped, her packages falling outward and she inward. Two of the packages fell between the moving door and the wall jamming the door shut, the Vulakin and four others were caught inside the door.   With the only exit blocked, everyone inside would have to wait until the packages could be removed. An alarm sounded, the guards rushed to attempt to remove the packages but were not able and therfore had to call for workers of the terminal to clear the door.

Maradish hailed an air taxi, entered the taxi and turned to look at the confusion and what if anything happened to the Doltic. She saw him standing inside watching as the taxi lifted off the ground. Without turning around she said, "Grand Royal Hotel!"

"YES 'm; the Grand Royal."   As the taxi was well off the ground before Maradish settled back for the trip to the hotel.

"Mara, don't worry about the Doltic, he knows where you are suppose to be going and will follow later." "WHAT DID YOU SAY?" She nearly shouted at the driver.

"I said Mara, don't…."

"NO one calls me Mara, but.." She interrupted.

"No one but me," said the driver as he turned around to look at her, it was Stafic!

She screamed with delight and jumped toward him but the small window between them prevented her from touching him.

"Easy now," Stafic continued. "You will just HAVE to control yourself for a while longer. Will be at the hotel in five minutes, have some things to say and not much time to say them."

"OK! But When I get a hold of you, you had better be ready."

"We want the Doltic to know exactly where you are until the right time for you to disappear," Stafic continued as if he did not hear a word she said. "You are to continue with your sales of the exotic foods as planned. Your contact will let you know when it is time to disappear."

"How will I know the contact?"

"That I don't know, I only know YOU will know."

It seemed to Maradish she had heard almost those exact words before. They arrived at the hotel, she received her room and unpacked her luggage, made arrangements for meetings with the officials concerning the food required and wanted for the banquet. The banquet was scheduled for three weeks and already the pace of preparation was becoming hectic.

XI

About a week after her arrival, while she was in the hotel restaurant calmly having her meal there became a sudden turmoil and a lot of noise in the lobby. There was a running around, yelling orders and general what appeared mass confusion. There were shouts, "Its' the QUEEN! The Queen!! MAKE ROOM FOR THE QUEEN!" Others yelling, "Roll out the purple rug! HURRY!" It all seemed as if this queen had arrived without warning and no one really knew what to do plus it was the "new bride" soon to be queen. Maradish got up from the table to see this "queen"?

The both of the front doors opened, in marched an entourage of individuals, there was a flurry of bows and shouts "YOUR MAGESTY", many were on their knees with their heads touching the floor. Through the door came a female dressed in royal robes with attendants all around and in front clearing a way for her.

Maradish looked at the queen, she seemed vaguely familiar, there was something about her? It was Chabmoda! So this is what she and Stafic had meant when they said she would know. She was not the greenish color but more of a pale tan but the face was the same, IT WAS CHABMODA! Her attention was directed toward the check in areas. There were shouts, " The queen requires an entire floor not a room! We don't care what you

MUST do, do it, clear the floor or the king will hear of your inefficiency and disrespect for a visiting Queen!"

For sure", thought Maradish. "She does know how to make an entrance."

It was later that day, Maradish was in her room when here was a knock and a card was slipped under her door. The card read, "Up the back way tenth floor, nine P.M."

Later as she entered the tenth floor, there were several individuals standing along the wall and Chabmoda waiting for her in the hall. The first thing Chabmoda said to Maradish was, "Don't worry about all these, there all males and they do not even see you and will never know if you were ever here." She could see the doubt on the face of Maradish so continued, "They are under my complete control." And continued. "I just thought we could have some time together before it all starts, who knows what will happen then."

"For the next two weeks as much information will be gathered about the upcoming wedding banquet as possible. Agents posing as various "guests", sales and providers of special merchandise, mingled among the general population, some disguised as a different species, if there was any possibility of discovery. Stafic is tp remain for the time being a Tyrunic, seller of expensive and rare gems. The intention is, whomever is responsible for this problem will know where you are but will not know how or exactly when you will make your move. For all intents and purposes, you are about to vanish into thin air and will reappear at your convenience sometime before or during the banquet."

"Plans are being made, modified, cancelled and different plans submitted, as new or different information was received and verified from agents scattered throughout the city. A consistent observation is; the day the king marries his "new" wife, it WOULD be followed by a lavish banquet at the largest banquet hall in the city beginning exactly at eight in the evening. The banquet would be attended by all the dignitaries, government officials and several hundred other guests."

A rumor which continued to surface but could not be positively verified was a royal someone, possibly some king and of course myself as a visiting queen, would also be in attendance. Another strong rumor we have been spreading is the assassination attempt of the king and all his family at the wedding before the wedding takes place. Rumors of this kind were not unusual, nearly every king or head of government had to contend with these types of rumors from day one. Although it may have originated as a leak about the attempt, not one "plan" from the agents has been ever considered it be done at the wedding ceremony. You will suddenly vanish in one week."

A week passed quickly, Maradish suddenly disappeared and could not found in the hotel or anywhere she normally had been previously. She was now in a secret area, being briefed about the banquet hall, the floor design, where and when to best avoid security persons and the known security systems. The hall was a three story building, inside was a large auditorium and two sides was rooms and closets used for storage and the dressing rooms, a third was the stage and the fourth were several entry doors. The rooms were used for the various entertainment acts which performed from time to time and remained empty between times. The auditorium could easily seat five thousand individuals. Security sensors and cameras were in the building but their locations were unknown and well hidden.

She tried to wear armor designed to cover most of her body but rejected it because it restricted her movements and ability to use her stealth effectively. She did select the weapons, offensive and defensive which easy to carry, did not make any type of noise when carried and a sufficient number to accomplish the job at hand. The other agents of the team involved have infiltrated the crowd and would only add firepower when verification of the target was made and the operation began. It was a process which had been successful for centuries.

With the possibility of another "king" involved, verification became all the more important, to eliminate the wrong head of state or the head of state of another member would not be acceptable by the Empire before or by the agents. Maradish had to be close enough to determine which was the target and which to be protected from harm.

For reasons she could not understand, Maradish had an uneasy feeling, almost to the state of nausea when discussing the operation. She had not had these feelings since the very first of the many operations she had been a part of to date, even her sleep times has became more restless than before. She felt as if she was a rookie on her first assignment. She thought maybe it was because the opponent KNEW she was here and just waiting for the opportunity to "get her" and once the operation began the opponent would be able to SEE her every move and what was at stake if anything went wrong, the number of her colleagues and friends whose lives were dependent on the outcome of this operation.

As a professional she was, she would have to or at least try, as she always did, to put the consequences of her actions out of her mind and not think of them again until the operation was completed.

As day drew closer, the feelings only intensified, until the night before the operation was to begin. She was very restless, even Stafic who was always able to calm her, could do nothing, she even became angry with him and began to glare intently at him. Knowing her what she was capable of doing, he stopped trying and remained quiet, watching her struggle in her discomfort.

It was morning, the sun had been up for about three hours, Maradish started to get dressed for her "work", along with Stafic she would leave in about another hour for the first step in the operation. They were to proceed to a wooded area a distance from the banquet hall, Maradish was to be left there with four backpacks of weapons, explosives, etc. and she was to work her way to a road leading to the hall. By doing so she would be between the guard station check point and the hall, the "musicians" after clearing through the check point would pick her up and transport her into the hall. They were due to clear the checkpoint during about the afternoon eating period.

It was only three miles from her dropping off point and the road. It normally take her no more than ten minutes to walk to the road, the others from the checkpoint to the pickup point was less than four minutes but were not due to come through the checkpoint for several hours. This would give Maradsih plenty of time even if she encountered any unforeseen obstacles to arrive at the pickup point with the backpacks and hide what would not be carried into the hall in a safe place to be pick up on the way out. An unknown factor was how long it may take the guards to "check" in coming vehicles. It would take an untold length of time for them depending on how through each check.

The unknown for Maradish was any hazards or obstacles she may encounter on her way including animals and any plants of a hazardous nature. However it still should give her plenty of time. She checked her watch and set her direction device and entered the trees. The direction devise would keep her on a more or less on a straight path to her destination. After only a short distance she encountered the first obstacle, it appeared to be a nearly solid stand of trees, bushes and vines forming nearly a solid wall in front of her. Her main concern was to find a way through the trees and especially the bushes and vines. Some of the bushes and vines had thorns. In some cases, the thorns were poisonous and if she were to be scratched, the result could be sickness or even death. Not knowing what kind of poison, there would be no one to assist with an antidote. She would not be able to carry every type of antidote, thus even a minor scratch would be fatal.

Therefore a slower and more careful movement through all the plants HAD to be made.   Carefully picking her way through the wall of trees, using what she had, she pushed her way around or away from her any suspicious plants but kept her bare hands and face clear, just in case. Through the wall of trees, which took almost ten minutes to penetrate, she entered mostly trees with scattered underbrush.   Growing in close proximity to each other, she was, at times, barely able to squeeze between the trees. She had to remove, very often, everything she was carrying, pass them through the narrow openings and then squeeze through herself. She would be confronted with the next pair of trees and need to repeat the process again and again. So it was, one step at a time until she finally reached the road exhausted and sweaty. She hid in the underbrush and among the trees the additional weapons and explosives.

After over two hours of a difficult "walk", just inside the tree line she hid herself to rest, eat the small lunch she had, wait and cool off. The "musicians" were still not due to arrive for more than an hour.

When they came, she retrieved the weapons, gave them to the musicians, got into the vehicle and they all continued to the banquet hall. As soon as she was picked up, she removed her "work" clothes, dressed as one of the musicians, along with the weapons placed inside and among the musical instruments she stayed with them until they were all safely inside the hall.

Once a group or individual was checked by the guards, anyone entering the hall would be considered part of the "cleared" group and were paid little or no attention. At the first opportunity, she and another female "musician" left the group, supposedly in search for a place to "freshen up".

They found an unused storage room on the third floor where she could again "get ready" for the operation, out of sight of all the arriving waiters, cooks, etc. The guests, dignitaries and others coming to the banquet would begin to arrive in another six hours. The meal would not begin until after the arrival of the king and his "new bride" and the king gave his usual speech. Although scheduled for eight o'clock, depending on the length of his speech it actually might later, sometimes MUCH later. The other king was due arrive before, how much before was not certain and he would be escorting the "visiting" queen because neither were supposed to have a spouse or mate.

Maradish could do nothing except wait. She set her time piece for an hour and thirty minutes before the scheduled arrival of the primary target, found a fairly comfortable place to relax and tried to rest. What she still had, even after the difficult passage through the trees was the restless feeling but she finally, almost exhausted she fell asleep. It seemed to her only a few seconds had passed before the soft buzzing of her clock woke her. She dressed in her work clothes, checked the weapons, set on stun and safeties on and other items secure against any noise or prematurely fallen free. She realized, they either knew where she was already or would soon know when she left her "hiding" place. It was very unnerving to be out of her element, to approach the "target" in a lighted or even semi- lighted area. As soon as she stepped out of the room, she would become the bait in a trap in which there was no information, not even who may be setting the trap or even if the individual would be present.

With only a hope that the trap would prove to be successful it was now was the time for the bait to be placed in the trap. She slowly opened the door slowly and only enough to slip out. She began to wonder why she was being so cautious, if they or it, whomever it or they might be, already knew where she was and watching her every move. Then she thought, might as well put on the show that is expected, give the impression and act as if she did not realize there were cameras and detection devises monitoring her progress. They WERE supposed to be a heavily guarded secret.

She stepped out of the room and the first thing she noticed was; third floor was very dimly lit. For sure it was to "make her feel at ease". Keeping herself close to the wall, staying in the shadows as much as possible, she slowly made her way toward the stage area. If they wanted a show, she was going not disappoint. The first staircase she came to, she thought of maybe to do the unexpected and go to the second floor. The second floor was well lit therefore with the thought of being forced a certain direction, she remained on the third floor, from her present vantage point she could see guests arriving.

She could hear the clamor of waiters, servers and all the others from below there appeared to be a rush to set the tables and gather all the necessary items for the banquet, it was now about an hour before the king was to arrive. Those arriving, of course, were the lower and less important individuals mostly invited only to fill the hall. Many of the guests believed they were "somebody" but in reality were only there to occupy a space and fill the hall.

She listened to the clamor of table and chairs scraping across the floor, dishes and utensils being set on the table as she slowly made her way to the next staircase. It was nearly dark with only a couple of dimmed lights. The last staircase was further away so she cautiously went there, it was brightly lit, impossible to use without being observed. Whoever it was wanted her to descend the other stairs, so she went back to oblige. From her position at the top of these stairs she could observe the activity on the floor and see the stage. The stage was nearly empty with the exception of a single large chair and a slightly smaller one next to it. That would have to be the "thrones" for the king and his "new bride". On the floor from the doors to the stage was a wide open path, no doubt the path the king would take to the stage. She also noticed there were guards stationed every few feet along all the walls, the king must believe in being well guarded.

In the shadows, she watched as guests continued to arrive, she would need to wait and watch for her target to arrive. She had arrived at this position, early, she COULD nothing but wait, remain in the shadows and hopefully not seen by accident.

Guests continued to arrive, the musicians were busy "tuning their instruments", she knew the musicians were agents, she had no way of knowing how many of the guests might also be agents how many of the guests might be also.

The instruments came to life with a sudden and very loud sound, it almost caused her to jump. Everyone in or close to the doorway cleared the space, rushed into the hall, turned and began to bow down and began to chant , "Hail to King Staufus! Hail King Staufus!"

Maradish thought, the name of the king was Faitisha, was this other king? Why was he here earlier than expected? If this was the VISITING king, it would make her job easier. She would just have to wait until the other king arrived.

Curiosity was almost over whelming, but cautiously, she watched the entry of the king. With him and arm in arm was another, it was a female dressed in royal attire. This had to the visiting king and queen.

The musicians were the only ones standing as they played the entry music, all others were on their knees, bowing down, heads nearly if not touching the floor. The king along with the queen were followed by an entourage of attendants as they marched proudly to the stage.

There were attendants surrounding the pair as they made their way up the steps and on to the stage. The pair sat on the "thrones", they had several armed guards on the right and left of them. As soon as they were seated one of the attendants shouted, "ALL RISE!" There was a the noise of shuffling feet, moving chairs and tables as over five hundred "guests" rose to their feet.

An attendant then shouted, "QUIET! THE KING HAS AN ANNOUNCEMENT!" Five hundred individuals suddenly became quiet, not a sound was heard not even a scrape of a foot.

The king rose to his feet, the queen remained seated. "Hear you all! King Staufus and his bride have gone on an extended honeymoon journey. I have been left to watch over you. We are now going to enter into a new and more prosperous life." There were cheers and applause from those on the floor of the hall. It lasted for minutes until the king raised his hands, quiet once more was attained without any effort. By the time the king raised his hands for quiet. Maradish began to descend the dimly lit stairs, she determined this is the one which needed to be eliminated. The king continued to speak of the great things he was going to do as king, interrupted several times be cheers and applause. I along with several others have formed an alliance to protect and prevent intrusion into our affairs by any other outside force.

Maradish had reached the bottom of the staircase, was about to release her weapon from her holster when he said, "To show you how I will keep that promise..." He shouted "NOW!" A net suddenly seemingly came from nowhere, pulling her off her feet and into the air nearly upside down. Just as sudden, there were six guards around her with weapons drawn and aimed directly at her. "This," the king continued. "Was from that outside force I mentioned. Sent to disrupt our peaceful life and assume control of your lives." From the crowd there erupted a chorus of boo's and chants of "never". "There are about ten others in among you who are confederates of this one, wanting only to destroy you and take control. I say, find them and kill every one of them! This one is MY prize."

He turned to face Maradish, "A HA! My pretty! You are now mine."

Maradish still upside down and wrapped in the net, looked at her capture and shouted, "NARVITA! What are you doing, we are on the same side."

"WERE! I have wanted you for so long but I had to get THAT blue thing out of the way. Unfortunately it required the destruction of the Organization to do it. It took years planning and convincing that the Organization was to powerful and needed to be dissolved. As a reward for a job well done THIS entire planet and you are mine."

"NEVER!" Shouted Maradish defiantly.

"Oh! You hurt my heart" Said Narvicta acting dejected. "You may say so now but you will come around to me and we will have such wonderful off springs. I will dress you in the finest of clothes, we will eat the most exquisite food and drink the finest wines, you will be happy and give as many offspring I desire to prolong my dynasty forever. You'll be a dutiful queen and bow to my every whim."

"You must be dreaming, I will never be anything but someone seeking a way to kill you."

"But my dear you forget, I controlled you once before and I can very easily do it again and I have improved upon my design. You will want to love only me and forget THAT blue thing forever. Besides what I will give you will be surgically installed so if and when I get tired of you I will just terminate you with a simple flip of a switch and find another." He then said to those guarding her, "Take her down. Be sure you remove ALL weapons, any communication devises and make absolutely sure you remove everything even if you must remove every piece of her clothing and have her stand in front of me totally nude. It WOULD be a great pleasure for me to see my future queen nude, I have seen her once already, so go ahead and remove every piece of her clothing!"

As the guards began complied with his orders, Maradish shouted, "You will soon be a dead king! One mistake and I WILL kill you!"

"Nonsense my love, your mistake was to be involved with that blue thing and not me, I had to try three times to get rid of him. Had to do it myself to get it done right, Taygo was just a bonus."

The guards had barely had the net off her when suddenly one had weapon in hand began to shoot the others. Nearly simultaneously, the guards stationed along the walls began to shoot and kill each other, chaos erupted as weapons were being discharged and uniformed individuals all over the hall were being killed.

Maradish stood motionless, not understanding what was happening, Narvicta appeared to had become a statute and unable to move.

"Maradish!" Shouted someone, it was the queen on the other "throne", It was Chabmoda! She was removing her royal attire, she was dressed as an agent underneath.

Maradish began to move and shouted," What is going on?"

"I will have to explain later but for now it is best to vacant the premises," she yelled back. "Help me take this piece of trash with us." Grabbing Narvicta by an arm and Maradish on the other arm the two females began to drag him toward the exit doors.

When the discharge of weapons began, many of the guests, females, who were standing listening, dove for protection under tables and behind chairs, the only things available. The male agents had fallen to the floor and covered their heads with what appeared to be a pillow.

With their own weapons in hand, the two were moving toward the doors, anyone with a weapon still standing was quickly dispatched. Several of the cooks, waiters and servers were female agents and joined the fray to defend their comrades. "Everyone stay down! Anyone so much as raises their head will have it shot off!" One of the male agents shouted, loud enough for all to hear as all the male agents stood to their feet. Those who happen to be still standing fell to the floor. Disguises of the agents came off and all began moving toward the now open doors.

As Maradish and Chamboda were dragging Narvicta toward the doors, she looked around the hall and it appeared that somehow over twenty five agents were inside the hall. She was almost surprised at the number but then again it was no surprise that was a large part of their training was infiltration.

Maradish and Chabmoda waited just inside the doors for several agents to proceed out first, if necessary, to provide cover fire for the exiting females, their encumbrance and the rest of the exiting agents. The sound of discharging weapons had alerted the outside guards and they had formed into a large troop headed toward the hall.

The first agents out, formed into a defensive posture and as the troop came into an open view and firing range, began to fire their weapons. Several died immediately, the first to die were those in the lead. The others broke ranks and scattered into the trees firing back as they did. Fortunately or unfortunately depending from which view point you are on, their shots hit no one but did damage to the building and other trees. Stepping aside, the females allowed more agents to exit to support the ones already outside. Diving and rolling to be behind any obstruction, firing at potential targets, the agents were soon outside and advancing on the troops scattered about. With years of experience and training the agents with systematic precision began to eliminate the opposition. Without leaders, those remaining with little to no training in tactics or maneuvers, were quickly eliminated.

Then agents quickly made a stretcher to carry Narvicta relieving the two females of their burden while Zennim and two others tending to the two wounded and one killed in the skirmish. OF the wounded, one badly burned and the other lost a hand, medical ointment was being applied to both and the wounds wrapped to prevent infection. A second stretcher was built for the badly burned agent. The one killed was also placed on the stretcher.

"Why take THIS thing with us?" Ask one of the agents pointing his weapon at Narvicta, " Let's just vaporize him right now."

Stafic and Taygo at almost the same time said, "He was one of us at one time."

"He gave that up when he tried to destroy us."

"Granted," said Taygo. "But there may be others involved and we really need to know who and high up the government line this conspiracy goes."

"OK. If you say. But in my opinion it is a waste of effort," said one agent. "Look what he attempted to do to us."

"Noted. When the time comes, you will have to believe, HE WILL be taken care of."

"Chabmoda, How long before he recovers before we can ask him a few questions?" Asked Taygo.

"Not for sure, I WAS very close to him and I was using a lot of my strength." She replied weakly and collapsed to the ground.

"Someone take care of her. She will need complete rest for at least an hour," shouted Taygo   "Make another stretcher, we really need to start moving toward the terminal," Said Datseric   "Gather up," demanded Prallian. "We need to be on our way to the terminal. No way to know for sure if the main military force has been alerted."

"Pick up all the weapons not damaged and check the storeroom for anything of value," declared Zennim. Agents hurried about and retrieved as many weapons and as much food supplies as possible before returning to the group.

They, without another word spoken, formed up a circle around the eight carrying the stretchers and the one wounded. The eight with the stretchers would have difficulty defending themselves.

"Maradish," began Brukist. "Need to know where the cache you hid before we picked you up."

"About a quarter mile down the road," she replied.

Two of the agents broke away from the rest and quickly moved down the road. They would be the advance alert of any potential opposition moving their direction. They moved through the shadows of the trees, trying to move quick as possible but remain out of sight as well. The five leaders were at the head of the group. It was slightly over ten miles to the terminal and the group as one person began to move.

The call issued all the agents not involved at the banquet hall, in code, to gather a half mile from the terminal. Most of them in this group were family members, the agents with them provided communications and protection, if necessary. With all the spouses, mates and offspring, there was a total of two hundred twenty five that would be assembling at the terminal.

XII

The meeting of the two groups was without any difficulty, they all came together on a small hill overlooking the terminal.. Two of the agents assigned for their protection approached the leaders. "We have important information," said one of them. "We need to tell you but it concerns every agent." The five leaders called for all the agents and they gathered together in a tight group.

"What is your report?" Ask Brukist.

"We intercepted messages from headquarters on Traket. It seems they knew or believe there was a takeover taking place here and this to be a staging point for a total government takeover. This appears to them to be verified by the fact the families and agents have disappeared. They are forming two massive forces, one to protect the capital on Traket and the other to put an end to any effort on our part to attack."

"THAT IS RIDICULOUS!" shouted several of the agents at the same time.

"Ridiculous or not, regardless, they believe it and the massing together the two forces is evident of their intentions, to confront or if necessary seek out and destroy every agent and our families. One more thing which may be of a more immediate concern. The military leaders here with the help of the "officials" of the Empire are gathering a force to seek out and engage us."

"We should not engage this force, our families will be to much of a target."

"Was anything said as how they found everyone including the families had disappeared?" Ask Datseric.

"Nothing mentioned that we could hear. It appears that someone in the Organization may have convinced them of the fact."

"Someone like this piece of trash?" An agent commented pointing to Narvicta.

"NARVICTA!" Shouted the reporting agent, astounded.

"We found out he was at least one of the instigators of the plot against us, may or may not be the central figure or if there are others involved. That we do not know." Said Taygo.

"The problem is not how it was done but exactly what are we going to do about," Said Zennim sadly. "Let's attack and stop this madness," cried an agent noted for a quick temper.

"THAT is exactly what they believe we are going to do," said Prallium the more cautious of the leaders

"Agreed!" Said Taygo. "We need to be somewhere we can rationally work out what needs or can be done."

"Not to mention," Said Brukist. "We are no match against any force in the environment of space. We don't have the firepower to win. On the ground we can hold our own against a much superior force in numbers, but in space we would be like a lame bird ready to be plucked."

"Of course you are right," Said the quick tempered agent. "I lost control for a moment." "Understandable. Our first concern is to be inside the terminal, that will at least slow down any airborne confrontation," advised Zennim. "We can handle a ground offensive but we don't have any defense against airborne ones."

"So what are we going to do?"

"First get away from this place. We will need transports for all our families," Datseric said pragmatically. "We have our supply ship and there should be a transport or hopefully more loading or unloading at the space dock," Suggested an agent. "We need to know what is available and take control of as much assets as possible to get everyone off this planet," Stated Datersic

They were watching the activity in and around the terminal and saw nothing unusual but they knew that did not mean a thing when there could be hazards inside, out of sight.

Chabmoda recovered enough to hear how most of the discussion progressed and she heard Taygo say, "We need to know if there is any opposition inside the terminal waiting for us. It is a restricted space and they could easily either move the shuttles out into space or destroy them before we could reach and secure them. It would isolate and confine our abilities to resist and overcome any opposition."

"How we can we get inside without being detected?"

"I'll try and close enough to see any activity," Volunteered Maradish.

"You would not even have a chance to get close to the front door with all the lighting."

"Not the front, I could see if there is a side door or access point."

"I will go", Said Chabmoda. "I'll can walk through the front door and neutralize the males."

"You are in no condition besides how about the females? We will have to find another way,"

Said Taygo.

Chabmoda sat up and looked at Taygo, Taygo suddenly said, "I guess that is the only way, go ahead."

Maradish had NEVER known Taygo to change his mind that quickly, suspected Chabmoda had influenced the decision somehow. Almost before Taygo had finished speaking, Chabmoda was up and running down the small hill to the terminal. Maradish moved quickly and was soon running close on her heels. The other female agents although surprised of the quick change of the decision and actions of the two, did not consider it was unusual . They watched as two females agents ran down the hill toward the terminal and all the male agents appeared to be frozen in place. Both females stopped at the corner of the building, while they caught their breath Maradish said softly to Chabmoda, "You must TEACH tell me how you do that, it could come in very handy."

Chabmoda smiled, "You either have it or not, can't teach something you don't know anything about." "There looks like a access door over there, give me five minutes to get in and set, I'll cover you as quick as I can get into a position."

"Five minutes."

Maradish quickly moved to the door, found partially buried in dirt and overgrown with weeds. With difficulty, she finally opened it just enough for her to squeeze through. Inside she found the floor littered with papers, boxes , pieces of wood and metal and a multitude of webs. With the knowledge of knowing there were many Dacifides, (a ten legged spider type) with a fatal bite, she had to be cautious not to get very close, there were some that would jump if sensed any potential meal. There was a ladder to her right, it may lead to a better view of the interior of the terminal.

Pushing aside all kinds of debris, some boxes which appeared to never been opened, curiosity of which almost made her to want to know what was inside but she pushed forward and up the ladder to the apparently a second floor. Through deep dust and still more debris she reached what seemed to be a window to observe the entire floor of the terminal below. Huge glass windows was the only thing separating her from the interior of the terminal. The windows were so covered with dirt and dust it was difficult to observe any movement below. She searched quickly from something to clean an area and found a discarded cloth of some kind and hurriedly tried to clean a small place on the window. She managed to remove enough dirt in time to see Chabmoda walk calmly through the entry doors. She cleaned more and saw several guards on a platform above the entry and exit doors. They were sitting around, very casually talking and drinking some kind liquid. From their position, they could observe the entire lobby but not be seen by anyone entering the terminal.

Had they been notified of the trouble at the banquet hall or were they only to act as if nothing happened for some reason? She wanted to call out to Chabmoda but even if she could hear it would also alert the guards. The small section of the window she was peering through and the thickness of the glass prevented firing even a warning shot. All she could do is watch helplessly as Chamoda walked into the terminal. All she thought of was to attempt to find a way into the terminal and finish anything that was started.

A quick look around, the only access to her present location was the ladder. With only a few jumps she was once more on the floor, there were the sounds of weapons being discharged when reached the floor. She saw what might be an access door to the lobby. She leaped to the door and began pushing the it open, it took a lot of strength to open, apparently it had not been used for a very long time. Opened enough to get through she literally jumped into the lobby, weapons drawn and safeties off. What met her eyes almost made her mouth drop open with amazement. Chabmoda was standing very quietly in the lobby, in a place of total view of those on the platform, but they were making no sounds.

"As we say on my world," Shouted Chabmoda. "Come on in, all is well, my man will serve you, but in this case just, come in, all is well. We need to call the rest to come on in."

"What about…."

"No worry," interrupted Chabmoda. "They were making so much noise when I came in I simply ended their good time a little early."

Both females went back outside and signaled the rest to come in.

The first to arrive were the leaders, followed by the families and surrounded by armed agents. Each leader began to issue orders to various members of their teams to secure the area and prepare for the attack of the coming military. Twenty were sent to secure any and all shuttles, clear each one of any supplies being loaded or unloaded to make room for passengers. Find out how many transports were in dock and use a shuttle and any means necessary to secure as many as possible for use. Another ten were designated to place anti- personnel explosives a short distance from the entrance and proximity explosives at various places around the entrance and any other accesses that could be used. They were to use enough to slow any advance long enough to move the families first to any transports made available. With the efficiency of a well oiled machine each task was preformed. Barely had the explosives been placed before the approaching force was seen. The arriving force was approaching on air vehicles, all the agents outside quickly retreated inside the terminal building. The battle was about to begin and would only end no one knew for sure.

The arriving vehicles landed outside the effective range of their weapons, discharge the occupants and they began to form up into an attack posture. The agents had taken positions inside using any protective material they could find to protect themselves. The families with all those in the terminal at the time were hustled as far away from the entrance as possible and using tables or any other items available to form at least some protection of any stray blasts of weapons.

All those considered noncombatants and not family members were hustled into a more secure area away from the possibility of being injured. Family members were being placed on the available shuttles and removed the transports.

The military force, outside, using the vehicles as shields began to advance on the terminal. They moved slowly until the first one encountered an anti- personnel mine. The explosion not only killed the one stepping on the mine, it severely wounded several others. The explosion indicated they were within range of the weapons the agents had and the fire fight began. The first blasts disabled the vehicles, eliminating the shields. Without the shield, more became vulnerable to the accurate and deadly fire of the agents.   The attacking force retreated to a safe distance. The knowledge of the possibility of more hidden mines a different tactic had to be employed.

The agents knew another tactic would be developed, retreated further back into the terminal, leaving only a token rear guard to resist. The tactic believed would be employed was to avoid anti-personnel mines by airlifting the soldiers all the way to the entrance. The proximity explosives were more powerful and carried more shrapnel . In addition to the ones already outside the entrance several more were scattered about in a haphazard fashion so a pattern could be determined. With a limited number of explosives available the agents were being cautious as to where and how many were being placed. The object was to slow the advance of the attacking force enough to obtain and execute an orderly departure as much as possible.

Before and while the first skirmish was taking place, three shuttles had been commandeered, two of the shuttles were used by agents to take control of the two transports in dock and there were only a limited number of family members on these two. The third was being loaded with as many of the families as possible. The shuttles were designed to transport boxes and crates of material from and to transports in dock. The result was only about twenty five individuals could be moved safely at a time. The total delay of the force had to be at least six hours with only three shuttles, already there had been a delay of a little over one hour.

Taygo with a hand signal called Chabmoda to see him immediately. "Are you able to help cause a delaying action?" Asked Taygo.

"I am still a bit weak but may be enough."

"Take Maradish and a couple others and do what you can but don't injure yourself beyond repair."

"I'll do what I can."

"Maradish", Chabmoda began. "Need your expertise. I want to get as close to the force as possible." "I'll put on their dinner table."

"Well maybe not that close! I'll need assistance back, two more females."

"I'll go with you," Said V'E. "I can carry you there and back if you want."

"I can see in the dark better than any of you, I'll go too." Said Kithria.

"Great!" Said Maradish. "Lets all go out through the side access doors I came in through and circle around to them. I'll take the lead, just follow in my footsteps."

Chabmoda, Maradish and two the female agents, V'E a Juthypotic, noted for her superior strength and Kitho-ria, a Gortitic with known more than excellent eyesight, left the rest and with the stealth of which they were trained, eased out and moved toward a position regrouping army.

They slowly made their way through the night, Kith-rio spotting obstacles to avoid along the way until they reached a position nearly close enough to touch the one on guard.

Only in this position for a very short time before Chabmoda said very weakly, "OK hurry let's get back.   Need your assis…" She didn't finish, she passed out.

Without another word, V'E picked her and had her over her shoulder like a small rag doll and they were on their way back.

With a quick look the three others saw a chaotic scene they saw soldiers shooting and killing each other.

Kith-ria said, "Remind me if she wants ANYTHING or wants me to do anything to go ahead and do it."

"You don't have to worry about that. It only works on the males," Said Maradish.

"Then she ought to teach each of us how it is done," Said V'E without even a gasp of breath in spite of the a person across her shoulder.   The three, arm in arm and carrying Chabmoda returned to the others in the terminal.

"It may take a while before there is another force gathered but it WILL come," Said Maradish to Taygo but Chabmoda needs a lot of rest."

"For now, it does not appear there will be enough to form any kind of assault," Said Kith-ria.

"Great job! I am going to put Cabmoda on the next shuttle, she has done enough for the night."

Chabmoda was being carried to the shuttle, still weak but awake when she said to Taygo,"If Narvicta has not recovered enough to speak by now, I am sorry. I may have been to close and used too much energy. He will always be nothing more than a vegetable."

"When we leave, we will leave him here," Said Taygo. "This was supposed to be his reward for our destruction."

"Sounds like just rewards!" Said one of the agents assisting loading of the shuttle.

Word came that two transports and their own mother ship were now ready to receive everyone. Transportation began, first would be the rest of the families, most of the agents would remain to make sure all proceeded without interference.

During the lull in the fighting, two sentries were place to observe the approaches and the rest met in an open area to discuss their alternatives.

"We need time to discuss what exactly we should proceed," Said Zennium. "Are there any suggestions of how or where we will be able to accomplish this important discussion undisturbed?"

"I will say we may have only a day or at the most two to leave here," Said Brukist. "The Empire, the force they are sending, it may well be here in a day."

"May I make a suggestion?" Ask Kofata, a Nakakia. Nakakia were noted for their excellent memory, they could recall even minor incidents from many years before.

"You have our attention," Spoke Zennium.

"When I was in the department of treaties and concessions, the treaty with Zanphoric was reviewed. There was a clause in the treaty, for no apparent reason at the time and it stated that anyone violating the boundary agreed upon by accident must return to their own space within forty eight hours or risk destruction. This appeared to be ridiculous at the time with the accuracy of our and their navigation systems."

"What has that to do with us?" Someone ask.

"If we violate the boundary, it would give us hours to try and work out the answer."

"It may give us time," Said Pralliun, but continued. "IF and it is a big IF the Zanphoric will allow us into their territory, they could just as easily destroy us without warning."

"The clause says "by accident" if on purpose we would be subject to destruction unless we could try to call our crossing, let's say for political asylum." Said Kofata.

"We would HAVE to convince them we are not crossing into their territory for any military purpose; that it is on a friendly request of help."Said Brukist.

"That would be great provided they shot first, to ask questions later." Reminded Taygo.

"As I see it, we have little choice, stay and let the Empire destroy us or take the chance of survival with the Zamphoric, requesting political asylum," Said Datseric.

"I say we take the chance, " Said Taygo.

All five of the leaders agreed to proceed to Zanphoric and request political asylum and hope the Zamphoric will accept them and not just destroy them out of hand but if they did not the Empire would do the job anyway. The rest of the agents, although were encouraged to think for themselves also believed in and with their leaders, agreed it seemed the best alternative.

Suddenly the two lookouts ran to the group, "A large force approaching, appears to be several thousand and with it a sonic cannon." ALL but a few of the families were already on the transports, two shuttles were loading those remaining and the third shuttle was returning from a transport.

"If it is anything like the cannon we are familiar with, it will take about an hour to set up and depending omn the power source a half hour to be charged. The same charging time each time it is discharged," Said Brukist.

"That will give us barely enough time to finish loading our families and the other to return and begin to load the rest of us," Advised Datseric.

(The following was the discussion of the leaders plus several of the agents with special information, none of the individuals will be singularly indentified.)

"The return of the last shuttle will be close but enough room for the rest of us."

"The problem will be to hold off the force until all can be safely on the shuttle and off the ground, out of range."

"Where is the most logical place to fire the first round?"

"If I were to have one shot it would not be directly at the entrance."

"Why?"

"The entrance is believed to be heavily mined with explosives, it might clear the entrance enough for the troops to advance."

"My opinion it would be the wall on one side or the other of the entrance so they can advance around the known mined area."

"If we then place explosives on both sides off the entrance it may slow them down enough for us to execute our escape?"

"Possibly, the problem is we have not a lot of explosives left."

"May not need many, if they THINK the area is mined it may be all that is necessary."

"Split up the explosives and place what we have on the most probable areas of advancement and hope it will be enough delay to get all of us off this place and out of range."

The explosives were hurriedly placed along the possible pathways, the agents had just returned to the group as the shuttle which was in route landed. Not over a few seconds later, there was a huge explosion on the right side of the entrance and a huge hole emerged.

Acting as rear guard, several agents with their leader moved to engage anyone coming through the hole, while all the rest loaded onto the shuttle. It would be very close and uncomfortable but the alternative was worse, they had only to wait for the rear guard. The delay had to be a minimum of fifteen minutes, time to move to and enter the shuttle , the door to shut and be locked before the lift off to begin. To lift off before the door is shut AND not locked, would cause the door to open with any reduced outside pressure. Even only a hundred feet or less of altitude could be a disaster for the shuttle and everyone on board.

The first of the advancing troop climbed and jumped over the twisted metal and debris left from the explosion, they were engaged by the rear guard. The first few were killed instantly, the ones following retreated temporarily before attempting another assault. During those few moments, the rear guard withdrew enough to allow the next assault to engage the mined area. Explosions killed the first and wounded many of those close behind. The rear guard laid down a pattern of fire as they again withdraw, this time to the shuttle. Squeezing through the shuttle the door with difficulty, leaving items, weapons and Narvicta they had been carrying behind, the door was shut and the lock with a loud clank was secure. The shuttle then lifted off the ground as the first of the troops, who had carefully made through the mine field arrived but were seconds to late as the shuttle lifted out of range of the weapons they carried.

The three ships, loaded with personnel made ready for departure, the shuttles were sent a drift into empty space to preclude any on the ground of interfering with last minute preparations.

All was ready, the announcement was made via the radio, "Set coordinates as mentioned, each set direction in different initial course to rendezvous in one week. Engage when ready." The announcement was purposely broadcast over the radio in hopes the military force on its way would intercept the message and change direction and return to defend Traket. The actual coordinates were the boundary of the Empire and the empire of the Zamphoria and the time was four days.

Zamphoria is an area next to the outer area of the Empire. The Empire warred over the area century or more ago and was to a stalemate with huge losses on both sides before a treaty was accepted providing each with sovereign control over the present occupied area. The Zamphoria are generally peaceful individuals but have a low tolerance for anyone attempting the disturb that peace, will fight to the death to preserve their peace.

Basically bipedal but have six appendages, when using the lower four, was able to, run at a speed five times or greater than the fastest individual in the Empire. The governmental setup is not known but believed it to be a caste type system, once born into certain level of the population the individual remains until it dies.   What distinguishes one gender or one caste from the next is not known, these facts the agents and their families were placing themselves and their very future. The last factor unknown to anyone outside the jurisdiction of the Zamphoria was their technological abilities. Since the signing of the treaty the only contact between the two has been a limited trade of commercial goods crossing the boundary at very specific points and even only very specific items agreed to in advance.

Even these slight incursions were only if the ships to and from were not to be scanned by the receiving area before or during the flight.

Three days later, the two of the ships arrived at the rendezvous point, arriving from two directions and awaited the arrival of the third due within one day. The point was inside the boundary of the Empire and when all three assembled preparations would be made to cross into the buffer zone. The buffer zone was neither part of the Empire or the empire of the Zamphoria but was an area twenty four hours distance at normal cruising speed of a space craft so it would be able to adjust its flight and travel back into its own territory. Once in the buffer zone the craft was under to jurisdiction of neither and considered neutral territory to both.

"Received a communication. Seems it was discovered by tracing the trail of the jumps we were not headed toward Traket. They are now determining where we are at this time," Announced an agent of one ship to the other.

"The closest military appears still two days jump away though," Said the other. "Better inform all the leaders, it may be a very close, time wise, if the other ship is delayed any at all."

"Right on!"

The leaders on the two ships were notified and agreed to remain on position for as long as possible but if the third ship had encountered difficulty and undue delay it would just HAVE to do the best it could, the safety of those here would have to take presentence. Twelve hours later, the third ship came out a jump and after the necessary recovery time was informed of the possibility of an armed force on the way. The three ships, in a tight formation began the flight into the unknown.

Twelve hours after entering the buffer zone, a force of eight military ships appeared outside the zone. The three ships were still within firing range of the weapons but because of the neutrality of the zone did not fire. Violation of the neutrality may have started another inter galactic war.

From the time the three ships enter the buffer zone they began transmitting on all available frequencies the following message, "To any concerned. We mean no harm. Three ships with individuals and families, in the buffer zone, request political asylum. Repeat! We mean no harm. Request political asylum." The message was repeated over and over again as they went deeper and deeper into the zone. There was only one direction they could travel now, to turn back would mean instant death as soon as they were clear of the zone if not before if someone on the battle cruiser got trigger happy.. The three ships approached the edge of the buffer zone, they had not heard any response to their repeated calls for asylum. Suddenly a voice was heard in all three ships at the same time but on different frequencies.

"You are about to violate the sovereign space of the Zamphoria and will be destroyed if you continue. Turn back, this will be your only warning!"

Zennim shouted on all available frequencies, "All ships to a complete stop!" The three came to a halt, they were still an estimated hour from the edge of the buffer zone. "Zamphoria! Zamphoria! We mean no harm to you or your people. We only seek political asylum from the Empire," was the response. Absolutely quiet, there was no other sound on the radios. Hours went by and the radios remained quiet.

Taygo, after two more hours went by transmitted on the radio, "What is the consensus of opinion? If we turn back we will be destroyed, if we go forward we have been told we will be destroyed and we cannot stay here, we will use our supplies and die. Talk it over among those on your ship and return with any decision or solution in three hours."

Two hours later the radio suddenly crackled to life, "To those in the buffer zone. It has been decided, before entry into sovereign space, all weapons will be neutralized, those not able to being neutralized must be placed in a secure area. All radars, outside optics. electronics and engines , except what is needed to sustain life, MUST be turned off, only one radio receiver, set on one frequency, will be allowed to remain on in the event WE need to advise of anything. If this is not agreeable then access to our area will be rejected and you MUST depart from the zone immediately. If you agree, we have the capability to neutralize weapons without harm to any individual. You have thirty minutes to accept or reject."

"Before we accept or reject, if all electronics and power are turned off we will be adrift and the possibility of encountering a hazard becomes very evident."

"We will maintain the integrity of your ships and provide necessary avoidance of any hazards."

"Under those conditions we accept and will begin immediately the shut down off all electronics!" Was the response from all three ships.

"Very well. We will monitor and as soon as all is accomplished, we WILL move everyone to an area out of range of any probes."

The shutdown of everything mentioned began, it required only about an hour, the three ships were now blind and mute and at the mercy of an unknown quantity. Shortly after the last element was turned off there was a slight jolt and then nothing. "Are we moving?" Was the question on every ones lips or mind. Without any outside visual sense it was not easy to determine.

The radio suddenly crackled to life, "Secure all loose objects and individuals as possible, the first of three cizmecki will begin in thirty minutes and will be separated by five minutes."

"Cizmecki? What in galaxy name is cizmecki?" Was a chorus of individuals

"Have no idea, maybe a jump but have no way to find out just get everything and everyone secure as possible." Was the response from each leader.

"Three jumps all within ten minutes? Never heard of such before."

"How is it possible without any power?"

"We will be destroyed without power!"

"I don't have any answers, we will JUST have to trust they know what they are doing and get everything secure. It would take over six hours to revive the engines even to minimum power, anyway."

Even during the discussion there was a flurry of activity securing everything and everyone possible. Exactly thirty minutes after the announcement there was a huge jolt, there few items not secure went flying through the cabin slamming against any obstacle it the way. This jolt was followed by two more of a lesser intensity than the first.

"The next will be the landing of the ship, we will do our best for a soft landing," Was the next announcement heard. There was a sudden and loud sound of disapproval of the statement.

"A space craft can't just land on the ground!"

"Are they trying to kill us anyway, it can't be done!"

"What does it mean a soft landing, where and how?"

All five of the leaders tried to calm and quiet the others with little success. The uproar continued until there was another moderate jolt . The voice on the radio calmly said, "Most sorry for the landing. You may open any access doors and leave the ship. Outside you will find an area to live while discussions continue with the government you call Empire, concerning your welfare. We will soon have a representative of our world visit and tend to any of your needs."

The access doors which were actually the cargo doors opened. It was an unexpected sight that came into view. As those closest to the doors looked, they had landed in what appeared an open field but close to a large pavilion. If it had not been for the armed guards surrounding the landing area they may have enjoyed the scene much more. The field was lush green with vegetation, softly rolling hills, a gently flowing stream of water emptying into a crystal blue lake and a heavily forested area beyond. The field was dotted with a variety of colorful wild flowers, blues, reds and yellows.

The guards said nothing as the occupants of the ships came out, only pointed the weapons if any wandered beyond an undesignated perimeter around the area of the landing.

The pavilion was a large building, white and appeared from where they stood to be very well maintained.

The occupants of the three ships, at first cautiously stepped upon the soil of the planet but was soon following by the orderly exit of everyone.

The sky was clear but there was a clear indication of the planet having twin moons. The sun was warm and bright.

"I could really get used to liking this if it were not for those guards," Said one of the agents.

"You got that right," Said another.

"How did they land all three ships and so close together," Asked another

"That, I am sure they will never tell," suggested another.

The offspring of the agents began to run and jump, it was the first time they could really stretch their legs in a very long time and they were ready to take full advantage of the opportunity. The parents at first was going to restrict their movements but saw nothing of which might harm them decided to let them go and enjoy themselves. The guards would restrict if necessary.

Everyone was relaxing in the warm sun and enjoying the air when two strange looking vehicles appeared and landed not far away. From the first vehicle stepped six individuals, they walked on two legs but appeared to have four arms, they were thin in appearance with oval shaped heads. They all appeared to look alike except for a colored chest and head. The one in the lead had a bluish head and chest and the five behind it were pale yellow. The armed guards parted allowing the individuals to walk directly toward everyone.

Someone shouted, "HEY ! Stafic!, look a relative!"

The bluish individual walked to the group assembled and without introduction said, "I am required to speak with your leader, what is it called?"

"We call him our leader but we have five of them," Said an agent.

"Then I will speak to all five, summon them, NOW!" It did not sound like a request but more like a demand.

"Brukist, Taygo, Zennim, Prallun, Datseric!   YOUR presence is needed over here." Said the agent sarcastically, slightly irritated by the tone of the voice. The five were already making their way to the location.

The Zamphoric stood nearly motionless with other five directly behind also motionless.

By prior arrangement between them, the five leaders along with the top agents all arrived together, bowed their heads and held out both their hands, not actually familiar how to greet this race of individuals but decided to use a sign of submission. Immediately the guards moved between them with weapons pointed at them. Datseric, with the longest time as an agent and leader, designated the spokesman for the group said, "We are most sorry. We did not intend to offend or cause concern. "My name is Datseric, I am designated as spokesman for the group. We mean you no harm." "Ack Ni flum orte mahgh zi ra ti, " Said a voice behind all the guards. Instantly the guards once more parted and the Zamphoric stepped forward. Please excuse the reaction, they are to protect and gesture not understood by them causes an instant reaction. My name is not important. I have been sent to introduce you to the Bak-maar-loit, the only one who speaks to and for the Majakquer. What he speaks is the way it will be with no discussion or questions. As soon as he spoke he turned, three of the others lined themselves on one side and he and the other two on the other. Bowing their heads, from the other vehicle came one similar except for the color, a dull silver, flanked by six others, all with the pale yellow like the previous ones. He walked straight to the group, stopped and began to speak, "The word from the Majakquer is; As prisoners of Zamphoria you will remove all personal items from the ships, you have one day, the ships will, according to the treaty will be returned to the boundary. This will be your home until further notice."

As soon as he finished speaking he turned, along with the six and without comment, show of any emotion or another word walked back to the vehicle, entered and left the area.

The bluish Zamphoric said, "The Majakquer has spoken, you have twenty four hours. You may now proceed to the building, there you will find food and drink for everyone and also in will serve as a place out the elements." He also turned and began to walk back to the vehicle in which he arrived.

"WAIT!" shouted Datseric. "We have a few questions!"

The bluish individual continued to walk ignoring the shout as if it was totally deaf , enter his vehicle and was gone.

Another vehicle arrived different from the first two. As with the first but different colored, five that appeared larger but bright green, were out and looking around as if expecting trouble. The next out, slow and careful, was one with the color of red. With careful steps, it walked straight toward the five leaders but completely surrounded by the five. Without any salutation the one in red said, "I am Raakafum, your liaison between you and the grand Typilomin. I speak for him and only through me will you speak to him. My purpose is to inform you the ships of which you arrived must be sent back and be across the boundary in two days in keeping with the treaty. Remove any and all personal items you wish to keep. If you have any questions I will attempt to answer them. But if there is any questions of your status and the status of the ships, that is already been determined and is law."

"We have some questions to ask!" Said Datseric.

"Very well, you may ask."

"What is the meaning we are prisoners?"

"Was the wrong word said? You will not do or go anywhere without prior approval, is this not what, prisoner means?"

"Well.. Yes. But we didn't come to be prisoners, we ask for asylum."

"When you PURPOSELY crossed the boundary, you were in violation of the treaty. When violation of a treaty occurs it is an act of war, therefore you became prisoners due to an act of war."

"Does that mean then as a prisoner, as you say of war, there may be a time we may return to our own countries?"

"That to is, I believe, the definition of a prisoner. Until that time, this will be your home, suggest you make the best of it possible." The Zamphoric spoke to one of the others with him and a device was brought to him. "This is for you, if there is any need you have call and we will attempt to provide. All your electronic devises will depart with the ships." The individual turned to leave and when Datseric and Brukist attempted to follow they were instantly blocked by two of the others with might have been some kind of weapon and apparently sent along to guard.

The two left standing, all six were back on board and the vehicle lifted off the ground and in a flash was gone.

"Lets retire to the building, eat, split up in our teams then unload the ships and plan for a long stay, at least we know they will not be sending us back with the ships," Said Datseric.

After eating, each team split into members of each family began to retrieve any and all items from the ships including items that could be used as a weapon, which could not neutralized, such as knives and such.

\"We have no idea how long we will be here or even what they intend to do with us, so the best is to make the best we have. Plan to live your life time here," Said Pralliun sadly.

With the ships unloaded of everything possible to make their life as easy as possible, the five groups split up to discuss among themselves what if anything they could do IF they ever returned to their worlds or what they might do if had to remain here until the end of their lives.

It was later on the first day when the first of the food arrived. It came in a large container, lower from a airship which never landed, only hovered long enough to deposit the container and beginning the next day, it would deposit one and retrieve the previous one. This continued, precisely at the same time each day for the next hundred eighty days.

The day after their arrival the ships which they had arrived were taken and not seen again.

The next thing to happen which would cause everyone to believe their stay would be more permanent was: The solar disk which provided continuous warmth never completely disappeared below the horizon. It would descend to almost half before rising again to overhead and starting back down. This was a cause of no darkness, a primary need for some of the group to maintain a healthy body. This was reported to Raakafum, the building they were staying was very good but it provided with no area of any even semi-darkness, it was completely open on all sides.

"Is there anything that could be done for those in need?" ask Datseric, the spokesman. "We all have a this need but not to the extent of some."

"Do you have any suggestions, this problem is completely beyond our understanding?"

"Perhaps some type of building where they would be able to retire into total darkness?"

"I must discuss this with my superiors."

Two days later, Raakafum returned and demanded all individuals to "get in the building and not leave until further notice."

As the last one, grumbling and fussing, entered into the building, Raakafum once more said in a voice of authority, "No one is to leave this building for ANY reason, speak or even make a gesture to the workers now approaching."

Suddenly out of the trees surrounding the open field there appeared what appeared thousands of individuals, the color of each one was of a pale tan almost white. With only the sound of moving feet on the ground they came to the area between the pavilion and the lake. Moving with the precision of a fine watch, the area was cleared and different sized buildings began to appear. They grew from the ground as if they were some kind of plants.

Raakafum watched and explained, "These building are being built different sizes, the largest are for the families, down to the smallest for the single individuals. We will leave it to you to designate who lives in which. Each will have the ability to shut one area completely from the solar disk but still provide adequate ventilation for any enclosed. All will be completed before the disk is down today. I will remain to insure it IS done!"

All was completed, it what seemed to those watching, in a matter of hours. As soon as the buildings were completed, every workers gathered together one group and left the way they arrived with only the sound of feet moving on the ground. A place was assigned to each family and individuals according to need and size.

Maradish and Stafic because they were a couple, were assigned a building large enough for privacy but not much larger. Others who were couples were assigned a similar sized building. As they settled for what they considered to be either a very long stay or maybe a forever place to live, the problem arose what could be done to occupy everyone.

It was about a week later acquiring a place to live, Maradish began to at first hint about starting a family. As each day began, the hint became talk, Stafic gave reasons not at the present time but as the intensity of her talk increased, his reasons began to fall on deaf ears. It was about three weeks after they had moved into their "home", Staic was sitting outside watching Maradish. She was walking along the shore of the lake, somewhat despondent because of his refusal to grant her desire. She was wearing a very brief outfit with the look of silver metallic. It only covered her body from under the arms to the thighs. The outfit glistened in the sunlight, framed by her black skin which made it glow even more brilliantly, she was beautiful!

He got up and walked to where she was and whispered in her ear, "I love you so very much. If you would like to start a family, then yes, let's start our family."

The squeal of delight was so loud it almost broke his eardrums and Stafic thought the Empire itself may have heard it. "NOW!" She screamed. "Yes now!"

That was all she needed to hear, she grabbed Stafic by the arm and pulled him toward their "home".

The females of the group watched the couple and smiled or giggled at the sight, the males were puzzled by the goings on but understood later as their female counterparts explained to them in private.   Another thing which took place within the first weeks after moving into their new "homes", was the development of various outside projects to occupy themselves. Some began to learn to grow native plants for additional food and decorations, under the direction of a Zamphoria who explained how to grow various plants and which plants to stay away from. Others were learning to fish, restricted to the shoreline and ALWAYS under the watchful eye of guards. Still others attempted to acquire the talent of wood carving. In short, they began to be resigned to the fact they would be there for a very long time if not until they die. Life for the group as a group became routine but it was a life.

On approximately the hundred eightieth day shortly after the food delivery, a vehicle arrived. As the vehicle was landing a call was issued for the leaders by those observing the landing. From the vehicle came Raakafum surrounded by his guards. The five leaders and the top agents quickly gathered in a group, curious about the arrival of him, he had not been around for a long time, he rarely came in person. They did not have very long to wait.

Raakafum walked directly to the group and without hesitation began, "It has come time to return everyone to the other side of the boundary. Our informants have told us they no longer are seeking you, it is believed all were destroyed when they destroyed the ships we returned. We had placed upon the ships devises to indicate they were occupied. This was done under the direct orders of the Majakqued.   The organization to which you belonged has been completely dissolved.   You will be returned to the nearest planet within their boundary, from there you will need to return to your home planet on your own. Of course this will be without the knowledge of the Empire. It will be your choice as to who will be the first but we suggest those with families."

"May I ask why you are doing this for us?" Ask Datseric as spokesman for the group.

"First, because it was said to be done by orders from the Majaklquer but also our belief to take a life unnecessarily is repugnant.

"How are you going to get all of us back across the zone without them knowing about it?" Ask Zennim.

"I believe you call it smuggle? Am I correct, I am not well versed in you language."

"You speak quite well," Said Taygo. "Better than some of us. Yes, smuggle is the proper word. How many are you able to smuggle at a time?"

"We will be able to accommodate up to five at a time."

"How are you able to smuggle individuals into their area?" ask Heebtruia one of the top agents.

"That must remain a secret, I am only authorized to say we have been doing it for centuries, undetected. Also you MUST never mention the fact it has ever occurred."

"That I don't believe you will ever have to worry about. If anything is said about it would indicate it as one of the possible a number of agents and would be lead to the immediate search for and extermination of fellow agents."

"That was our thoughts as well, that is why we decided to return everyone to the other side."

"Why will you take such a risk?" ask Brukist.

"We do not want you here,"

Said Raakafum. "But more than that, the place from which you came waged a long war with us to try and take our land. Many of my people were killed therefore if there is ANYTHING we can do to "repay" that will a pleasure to us. They do not want you in their area so we thought that would be the best thing we could do "to help" place you back".

"What can you do for Stafic, he has no home to return to?" Ask Taygo. "And he easily identifiable as an agent and thus cause the search and destruction of the others."

"That we did not realize this problem, I will consult with my superiors. It may be several days, in the mean time determine the first to return, they are to take with them only what they are able to comfortably carry on their person. Seven solar days will be the first and every seven solar days after until all are returned. I must return now." Without another comment or word he returned to his vehicle and departed.

The first of the families was selected by lot. This began the exodus of all the agents. Raakafum arrived to observe the departing of the first of them.

"The superiors have made the decision that the one you call Stafic be allowed to remain on this side of the boundary, indefinitely. The land on which you now stand will be for you and if you have a mate or wife. You will be completely isolated. All contact with any of those on this side of the boundary as well as the other side as well. You will be left totally alone but before the last of the others leave if there is anything you can think you will need so inform us, once the last one leaves all contact with you will be broken."

"Those are very harsh requirements, as for me I must stay or jeopardize the safety of all the others but I must ask my wife, she is with offspring and I will not force her o stay."

"I am staying with you whether you like it or not," Shouted Maradish

"Well that settles that", said Stafic.

"Very well," Stated Raakafum. "I was instructed if acceptable to inform you, starting tomorrow and up the date last one leaves, if necessary, instructors will instruct you on growing plants and animals for you food. Food deliveries will cease. Also that thirty miles in all directions will called contaminated, no one will be allowed in or out the area. This is the word from the Majakquer, it is LAW!"

The families then the couple and finally followed by the individuals packed what they could, said their good byes, knowing they would not ever be able to even acknowledge the fact they knew each other

Stafic and Maradish stood and watch the last of the agents and all the guards leave they were now all alone, they had only their love for each to rely upon.

The Organization no longer existed, all the members arrived safely across the boundary and melted back into their own peoples. The Organization, its' agents, its' accomplishments, dedication of the members and any information relating to or about was systematically erased from all historical records of the Empire. The extreme secrecy of the Organization made the task relatively simple. There is only a minor footnote left in the history books of the Empire which read, "A group of individuals were helpful in expanding the Empire to its' present size."

(Completed February 10, 2025)